Yosemite Fortune

C. R. Fulton

THE CAMPGROUND KIDS
www.bakkenbooks.com

Yosemite Fortune by C. R. Fulton
First Edition
Copyright © 2023 C.R. Fulton

Cover Credit: Anderson Design Group, Inc.

All rights reserved. This book is protected under the copyright laws of the United States of America. This book may not be copied or reprinted for commercial gain or profit.

ISBN 978-1-955657-55-6
For Worldwide Distribution
Printed in the U.S.A.

Published by Bakken Books
2023

*To every treasure hunter,
may you find the most important treasure of all.
Do you love treasure hunting? Ask your mom or
dad to look up the Forrest Fenn treasure!*

National Park Adventures: Series One
Grand Teton Stampede
Smoky Mountain Survival
Zion Gold Rush
Rocky Mountain Challenge
Grand Canyon Rescue

National Park Adventures: Series Two
Yellowstone Sabotage
Yosemite Fortune
Acadia Discovery
Glacier Vanishing
Arches Legend

For more books, check out:
www.bakkenbooks.com

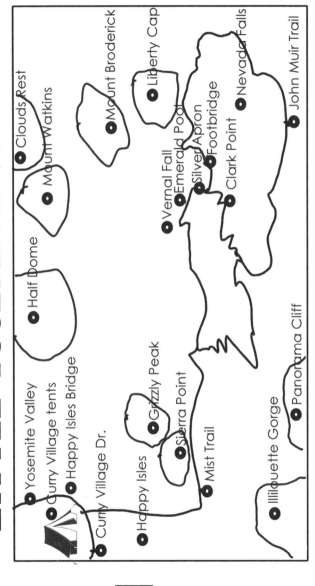

- 1 -

The attic ladder feels rough under my hands, almost like climbing a tree. Mom only lets me up here once in a blue moon, so I scurry up like a squirrel.

"Hurry!" my ten-year-old sister Sadie urges.

The unique scent of the attic envelops me with its mixture of stale air, dust, and...*discovery*. I balance on the rafters until I reach the small area with a solid floor where Dad stores our Christmas decorations.

"Don't make dust," I warn Sadie as she reaches for the poofy gray insulation surrounding our small floor. The ceiling isn't high enough for me to stand up straight, so I hunch over.

Sadie just smiles and sinks both hands slowly into the fluff. "Remember when I grabbed the pink insulation that you're not supposed to touch?"

"I'd rather not," I say, turning to scan the random piles of boxes.

Kneeling is easier, so I crawl toward the farthest corner and click on the flashlight I have clamped between my teeth. The first box I open is full of old baby clothes. I push it aside and reach for another, my fingertips tingling. *I've just got to find the treasure up here.*

The next box contains a wooden model of a car. I pick it up reverently and blow off the dust; it must have been Dad's when he was little.

"Just another minute!" Mom's muffled voice echoes through the small opening.

"Already?" Sadie asks.

"We've got to pick up Ethan in 20 minutes; then we're off to catch our flight to Yosemite!"

Mom's words send a thrill down to my toes, but I don't waste even one second. I lean down to search the bottom of the box. I lose my balance, shifting the boxes, and I gasp.

"What's this?" My subdued whisper, dampened by the heavy air, draws Sadie to my side.

"What's what?" Her long brown hair tickles my neck as I lean forward. One flap of a box protrudes from deep under the insulation. A slow-moving cloud of fine dust rises as I shift the hidden box closer. I hold my breath as I struggle with its weight. *A camouflage canteen is sitting on top!*

"Give me a little room," I mutter as I nearly plunk the mysterious box on Sadie's toes. She pulls mounds of soft insulation from the open top of the box, revealing several notebooks stacked unevenly. The first one has messy handwriting that says *Twice Buried, Once Found*. Sadie picks up the canteen, and I pull out a thick hunk of bronze metal.

"It's so heavy," I whisper in awe.

"Time to go!" Mom's muted voice from below barely registers in my ears.

"What are you?" I ask the heavy item that looks

like a thicker-than-normal metal hockey puck. I flip it over to see a clouded glass face. I suck in a long breath; mesmerized, I rub my thumb over it.

"Coming!" Sadie returns the canteen to the box and crawls toward the exit.

I linger, scowling at the device. A faint line reveals the possibility of a lid of some sort—if I could only figure out how to open it.

"Isaiah!" Sadie's sharp tone tells me she'd been calling for a while.

"Okay, I'm coming." The dusty cover of a small book in the box catches my eye. I snatch it as I turn to follow Sadie. I barely manage to get the device jammed into my pocket, and now I have to hold up my pants as they sag from its weight. By the time I'm back down the ladder, I can't contain the questions running through my mind.

"Mom, whose box was this in?" I struggle to pull the brass item from my pocket.

She scowls at it. "I've never seen that before."

"Can I have it?"

"It's not mine. You'll have to ask your dad."

"DAD!" I shout, but Sadie interrupts.

"He's not home yet. What's this?" She takes the book from my hand and wipes off the cover and reads *Real War Heroes, Stories for Boys*. She wrinkles up her nose and hands it back. "I call the window seat!"

"Ugh," I groan. Our 14-year-old cousin Ethan always gets the other window seat in the new truck.

"When will Dad be here? I thought we had to leave."

"We do. Hopefully, he'll be here in a minute or two. Isaiah, hurry and grab some gum to help with the pain of ears popping when we're flying."

I offer a crisp salute and take off for the kitchen. I can't wait to fly to Yosemite National Park! I run past the golden picture frame in the hall. Mom and Dad had planned our next five national park trips with one picture for each. I think I have been looking forward to Yosemite most of all. I careen through the living room and notice the television is still on. *Odd…we almost never watch it. Mom must've been checking the weather for our flight.* In midstride I see Dad's face flash on the screen.

Bewildered, time seems to slow as I stare at his gray stubble. *Wait! Dad's hair isn't gray!* I skid to a halt, my mouth hanging open as I stare at a man who is a perfect picture of what my dad will look like in 20 years. I see the same wide jaw; bright, blue eyes; and eyebrows that I never want to see lowered when he is upset at me.

"Um, Mom…why is Dad on TV?" The entire world has seemingly stopped spinning.

"What do you mean?" she asks as she and Sadie enter the room, carrying packed bags. They assume the same open-mouth stare that I can't wipe off my face.

"Elliot Elkland leads treasure hunters on a merry chase." She slowly reads the caption below the picture like she's in a dream. "Why is that name familiar?" The scene changes to a poem called "Twice Buried, Once Found."

"Hold on a minute!" I snap my fingers. "I've seen that phrase somewhere…"

A news announcer says, "Elliot Elkland released a clue last week, telling reporters that he's hidden more than $1 million in gold bullion, precious gems, and ancient coins. He says the finder will own the entire stash."

"What a strange day," Mom says, scowling at the screen as Dad's older look-alike reappears. "We've got to go; I hear your dad pulling in."

"A treasure map…" I whisper.

"A treasure poem…" Sadie corrects.

The reporter continues, "Crowds of treasure hunters have descended on Yosemite National Park, the Redwoods National Park, and other select locations in California. Activity has been intense since Mr. Elkland released this statement today, and I quote, "I've always loved the largest trees in the world. They are a treasure in and of themselves, and treasures are often hidden in public places."

"Yosemite," Sadie and I whisper together.

YOSEMITE FORTUNE

"Out the door. We cannot be late!" Mom calls as I hear Dad step into the house.

"I need 30 seconds, Mom!" I shout. My socks slip wildly on the hardwood floor. I leap for the thin string that will lower the attic ladder and miss it twice before it's in my grasp.

I scurry up into the intense quiet and once again fill my lungs with that exhilarating scent. I stretch for the notebook, blowing off a thick layer of dust. It makes me cough; but sure enough, I see the words *Twice Buried, Once Found* written on the cover. Possibilities run through my mind. *What are the chances of two different people writing something with the same name? Especially when Eliot Elkland is so eerily similar in looks to my dad?*

I scramble down the ladder, colliding with Sadie as she races by with the gum I was supposed to get earlier.

"Thanks," I say, then we run for the front door... and a most unexpected treasure hunt.

-2-

"Elliot Elkland is my great-uncle?" I nearly shout, making Ethan, who is sitting next to me, plug his ears.

"Hold on, Uncle Greg! You're saying that we're related to some rich guy?" Ethan asks, running his other hand through his shaggy hair. He's tall and thin, and his long legs are pretzel-shaped in the cramped back seat.

"Well," Dad says, "I didn't know he was rich. Truth is, I didn't know he was alive." He guides the truck into a parking spot at the airport.

Mom hurries us all along as we lug our bags toward the terminal. She alone notices the seconds ticking past that may result in missing our flight. Everyone else is focused on the treasure.

"My mom always told me I looked like Uncle Elliot, but I haven't thought about him in years. I do think I have an old box of his belongings in the attic."

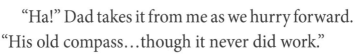

I freeze. A shiver runs up from my toes. *It can't be!*

"Was this his?" I ask, lofting the heavy brass piece I had found in the strange box in the attic.

"Ha!" Dad takes it from me as we hurry forward. "His old compass…though it never did work."

"Oh, Isaiah," Mom said. "I didn't realize you brought that along. It's too late to put it back in the truck. We'll have to put it in your checked bags and hope the baggage screeners let it through."

I had forgotten how picky the security guards are at the airport. "Sorry, Mom!" I say, hoping I didn't just ruin our entire trip.

She stashes the compass in my bigger bag that will ride in the plane's belly. She smiles at me. "It will be fine—hopefully."

"I am related to a millionaire!" Ethan is slouched forward with a look of amazement etched on his face as he strides along.

We rush through the airport doors, and I clutch the notebook and war stories book to my chest as Dad hefts my big bag onto a conveyor belt.

"What happens if they don't let my bag through?" I ask, thinking of all the important camping gear I've packed.

"I don't even want to think about it," Mom replies, pointing dramatically toward the far end of the airport. "But our plane starts boarding in ten minutes! We still have to get through security and make it to the farthest gate in the building to catch our plane!"

The employee takes the last of our large bags.

"Go!" Dad barks with a twinkle in his eyes. He loves a good challenge—just like me! We rush forward, our carry-on bags feeling heavier with every step we take.

"We've got...to get...our shoes off!" Mom is bending while running until she gets one shoe in her hand.

Sadie, always the most flexible, has hers off within two steps. Ethan's long arms promptly get tangled up in his legs, and he somersaults to a stop on the floor. I nearly drop my trusty backpack—the one with the bear-claw slashes and all my Junior Ranger badges—as I try to kick off my shoes.

Dad goes for a different theory, pulling ahead at top speed until he reaches the frowning security officer, then bends to unlace his big boots.

"Shoes in the bins, take everything out of your pockets and put it in the bin as well." The officer's frown deepens as one of my boots misses the bin and clangs on the conveyor belt.

"Sorry," I pant. It sure is difficult to let go of that precious notebook. I watch the bin inch away from me on the conveyor.

"4½ minutes," Mom whispers. I see the tense smile pasted on her face.

"Step through the metal detectors," the guard's voice drones out the words.

"Oh, boy..." another officer says as he stares at the screen as Ethan's bag passes through the scanner.

"Is that like, 'Oh, boy!' Or 'Oh, boy...'?" Mom's voice dips on the last words.

"Boy," The officer repeats slowly, and my stomach feels like it hits my toes. I elbow Ethan in the ribs after standing on tiptoe to see the screen.

"You really brought scissors on board a plane?"

He lets out a long breath with one finger in the air. "Um...there's a story behind that."

"We don't have time for a story," Mom whispers. Her fake smile grows larger as she makes this comment under her breath.

"Do we allow passengers to carry scissors on board?" The officer asks a third security guard.

"We'd better check the manual."

A squeak escapes Mom as more officers converge on Ethan's scissors.

"Let's see…" One of them flips through a black booklet. "Says here, scissors with a blade of under four inches are allowed. Anybody got a measuring tape?" A few of them pat their pockets.

"Nope. We'll have to call down to the office."

Mom steps forward. "I believe I can easily remedy this issue."

She picks up the scissors with two fingers from the bin under the watchful gaze of five security officers. Holding the plastic handle as if it were dirty socks, she walks to a large garbage bin and drops them inside.

"There…that was easy, right?"

The frowning officer crosses his arms.

"Are we now clear to proceed?" Dad asks, pulling his boots from the bin.

"Three minutes!" Mom shouts.

"I suppose." The officer turns to stare down the next passengers.

I snatch the notebook first thing, grab everything else, then sprint for gate 40 9E.

"Wait, please, sir!" Dad cries, waving our boarding passes at an airline employee far ahead who is sliding a door shut.

It's the same door that has our plane on the other side.

The man checks his watch, half his mouth tips up in a smile. "Five, four, three!"

"Oh!" Mom cries, rushing faster.

I didn't know she could run like that!

"Two!" the airport employee shouts.

Dad slaps our tickets into the man's outstretched hand.

"Bingo! I love it when folks beat my countdown!" He inspects the papers with a smile, then pulls the door back open.

"Welcome to Flight 467 to California."

The metal walkway to the plane feels strange under my socks. I clutch my boots to my chest, along with the books as we squeeze into the tight corridor of the plane. Ethan, Sadie and I get three seats directly in the middle of the plane. I sit and then contort as I try to get my boots back on in the cramped area. Uncle Elliot's notebook plops off my lap and into the middle of the aisle.

The sound draws the attention of four or five other passengers. I see one of them mouth the words *Twice Buried, Once Found.* They all lean forward with intense interest in their eyes. I snatch the old notebook and hug it against my chest. The passengers' eyes remain glued on the slim volume.

At that moment, the thought occurs to me that I'm holding a million dollars in my hands. *Maybe.*

-3-

I ease open the book, shielding it from the others' view. Then I read these words:

> Yell loudly on the drive; the North will be glad you did.
> Ogle the pointy peaks high above that have never left.
> Somewhere below lies one silhouette of George—white-haired and ancient like the clouds.
> Enter the fog, but only at the equinox will you draw near.
> Move beyond the desire for silver snow and go for the golden morning flare.

Yosemite Fortune

If you pass the curve, you'll reach the end, unsatisfied by half.
Turn aside from the common ground, Rick and Libby have done the same.
Encased in the cradle, 1001, though tiring, are not fatal.

My finger traces the words as they are seared into my mind.

"Let me see that," Ethan snatches the book and begins reading the words aloud.

"Shh!" I glance suspiciously at the other passengers. *I'm sure they're leaning toward us to listen.*

"What? This clue is plastered everywhere. It's not like it's a secret," Ethan retorts.

I shrug. "It just seems like something we should keep between…" I glance over my shoulder as the plane takes off, pressing us back against the seats. "You know, family." I whisper the last word.

"Hey…" Ethan lowers his voice and motions for Sadie and me to lean toward him. "Speaking of family, why was the baby ant confused?" He pauses for half a breath. "Because all his uncles were *ants*!" He leans back in his seat, holding his stomach as he laughs. Sadie and I look at each other and shrug our shoulders.

"I wish we could have asked Dad more questions about…you know," Sadie whispers.

"Me too, but no way am I talking across the aisle about something *this* important."

Sadie pulls an item from her pack. I reach for the map she hands to me.

"Oh, perfect!" I say, keeping my voice hushed as I unfold a map of Yosemite.

"Where's mine?" Ethan asks.

Sadie merely ignores him and continues studying her map.

"Are you disregarding my question on purpose?" he asks.

"Oh, sorry, Ethan. I thought you were joking, like always!" Sadie smirks, then throws back her head, laughing.

"Humph!" Ethan pulls a piece of saltwater taffy from his pack. When he opens the crinkly white wrapper, I inhale the scent of fake bananas.

"Shhooo…" Ethan says through teeth that will barely open as the taffy threatens to glue his jaws together. "Washhhh dat firsht line?"

I repeat it quietly as Ethan and I study the map of Yosemite.

"Are we even sure the clues are in order?" Sadie asks as she puts a stick of gum in her mouth. I grab some gum as well because chewing it will help balance the pressure in my ears from the plane's climbing so high after takeoff.

"Well, there is no legend on this map. So, I guess we'll just have to guess."

"Yell loudly. What good would that do? Unless it's a starting point or a cave where your voice would echo," she suggests.

"Or even a canyon; voices would echo there too," Ethan adds, swallowing his taffy and promptly reaching for another.

I slide my finger over the map with a sinking feeling. "Yosemite is sure full of canyons."

"What if it's buried in the redwoods?" Sadie asks.

"I shink meee shooo moo how."

"What?" Sadie giggles.

Ethan struggles to open his mouth, and this time the scent of blueberry invades our row. "I think we should go there too." When he reaches for another piece of candy, Sadie holds out her hand.

"I'll take one," she says easily.

Ethan slaps one into her palm, and my eyes go wide with horror. He realizes his mistake as he tries to snatch it back, fumbling it. The white-wrapped treat skids down the aisle. I put a hand over my heart and go limp in my seat. "That was close."

Sadie snaps her fingers in frustration as a flight attendant picks up the taffy. "Not quite close enough."

"Sadie, you would have been running on the ceiling of the plane if you ate that," I say.

"Mmmmm..." She studies the roof with a mischievous glint in her eye. "Sounds fun!"

Really, I know of no words to explain what happens to my sister when she eats sugar. Her body becomes almost superhuman, but her brain completely shuts off. *Sugar Sadie*...I shiver inwardly at the nickname.

The attendant hands Ethan the taffy. She leans in close, smiling. "Today, I feel like a schoolteacher."

We stare at her blankly, so she continues. "Only two people on this entire flight aren't working on that riddle." She points to my parents and then at the book in my lap.

I look over. They are holding hands, talking and laughing.

"They must be newlyweds," she adds wistfully.

"No, ma'am," Sadie says. "Those are our parents. They've been married since...forever."

"Really? That makes their relationship even more beautiful."

"Say..." Ethan says with a cheeky grin. "A schoolteacher usually gives out grades. Who do you think will receive the highest score?"

I can see where Ethan is going with this somewhat devious question.

The flight attendant's smile widens. "I'll let you know in a few moments." She scoots down the narrow aisle, making sure folks are comfortable.

The seatbelt lights turn off, and a big man, tall and heavily built, slowly makes his way toward the front. He's hobbling unsteadily, and one of his meaty hands grips each row of seat backs as he shuffles along the narrow aisle.

This plane has two seats near the windows, then a narrow aisle, five seats across the center, then another aisle, then two more window seats.

I flip through the rest of the notebook, finding only a few drawings here and there. None of us can figure out what they're supposed to be.

"Let's act like the clues are in order and see if we come up with anything." Sadie's finger runs over the map of Yosemite.

"Yell loudly. Yeellloowwd. Yellow. Do redwoods grow in Yellowstone?" Ethan asks.

"No. I already thought of that," an unfamiliar voice says from behind us. We all twist in our seats, peering through the cracks. A slim man shrugs his shoulders sheepishly, clearly regretting that he had made the comment.

We face forward, our eyes wide.

"It's as if Elliot Elkland has infected everyone with treasure hunt fever," Ethan whispers.

I hug the notebook against my chest, biting my lip. *How can we possibly beat all these other hunters to the treasure?*

The bulky man exits the forward restroom and starts the long walk back. This time, he hobbles down the aisle on my side. I notice that every time he lurches forward to reach for the next top of the seat, he carefully scans the passengers. A familiar twinge of danger races across my chest as I watch him coming toward us.

"Why won't shrimp share their treasure?" Ethan asks, but I can't tear my eyes away from the approaching man. "Because they're *shellfish*!"

The man who had commented from behind us snorts a laugh. Ethan smiles, nodding. "At least he gets it…and appreciates my humor."

The man's massive hand compresses the seat in front of me, and our eyes lock. That familiar sensation streaks across my chest again, and my breath comes faster as the man scans my lap. He frowns, and I flinch as he grasps the seatback above my head. I grip the notebook more firmly, wishing I had left it in my pack.

"I do not like that guy," Sadie whispers.

"Feeling's mutual," I mutter, curling forward, shielding the notebook. I open it as fast as possible, copy the clue onto another sheet of paper, rip it out and then carefully slip the notebook back into my pack.

The airline flight attendant stops by to tell us who has the highest score. "The man with the limp has four maps, graphs, and a satellite readout of the park, so he is the clear winner," she announces.

By the time the plane lands at Merced Regional Airport, we've marked our maps with important words from the clue. *Half* must stand for Half Dome, a massive granite rock that is one highlight of Yosemite. The word *cloud* probably stands for Clouds Rest, a mountain featuring a 14.5-mile trail by the same name.

"14.5 miles…" Ethan mutters.

He's right! Suddenly Yosemite's 1169 square miles of wilderness seem too large, and the chances of our locating Uncle Elliot's treasure are far too slim.

We shuffle along in the slow-moving line to exit the plane. Sadie grips my elbow when we reach the wide main concourse of the airport. "Look!"

People are rushing everywhere. "What?"

"That's the limping man!" She points, and I locate the big man. He's cutting quickly through the crowds *without a limp*.

Ethan crosses his arms. "I think this treasure hunt just became more interesting."

I shiver with dread as I watch the man scold two boys who are about Ethan's height.

"We're going to have to up our game here," Ethan declares. "We can't let *anybody* see our solutions."

"If we *had* any solutions," I say.

-4-

"Hang on," Ethan says as we pass the South Gate entrance to the park, inching along in the heavy traffic. "He is *my* uncle too, right?"

"Yes, Ethan," Dad replies patiently. "Your mom is my younger sister, so Elliot is your great-uncle as well."

"Whew," he says, going back to reading the clue.

"Dad," I ask, tracing the map of Yosemite. "Will we get onto Northside Drive at all?"

"No, I was planning to take Southside Drive. We can get to Curry Village faster."

"WHAT?" Sadie pulls her nose up from her map. Clearly her thoughts are the same as mine.

"But the first clue contains the words *North* and *drive*. We *have* to yell loudly while we're on it!"

I nod vigorously, hoping Dad will agree.

"Well…" Dad shrugs.

I don't think he's going to go for the idea.

"But what if something happens the first time you enter that you might miss if you don't follow the clue?" Ethan's voice is pinched the same way my throat feels.

We must find this treasure.

Mom turns in her seat, and seeing the stress on our faces, she says, "Greg, it wouldn't be that far out of the way to take Northside Drive."

"Well…" Dad waves one hand. "Don't you think we should get directly to our tent?"

We watched anxiously from the backseat of the truck we had rented at the airport.

Mom's eyes narrow. "Greg…" is all she says until he finally looks at her. "What is the real issue here? I thought you would enjoy the treasure hunt as much as the kids—maybe more."

He shrugs; but now, with eight eyeballs glued on him, he sighs.

"Uncle Elliot was, is…well…always an odd sort. I just can't imagine him actually having money in the first place, I guess."

"But you don't really know him at all—not since you were a boy."

"That's true. I mean, the last word we received from the Army was that he was MIA."

"Is that like the CIA?" Sadie asks.

"No, honey." Mom hides a giggle. "MIA means *missing in action*. MIA soldiers are lost during active duty, but the Army can't prove whether they are dead or alive."

"The whole treasure all sounds a little too farfetched for me," Dad says.

"Why don't you call your mom?" Mom prods.

"Okay, fine. I'll ask her." Mom dials for him and slips him a pair of earbuds.

"Hi, Mom," Dad says. "Did you know that Uncle Elliot was still alive?"

I sure wish I could hear Grammy's response.
"You did? I don't remember that."

We all lean closer, hoping to eavesdrop on the conversation.

"No kidding," Dad says; then he's quiet for a long time, listening.

I notice the traffic is becoming more congested, and suddenly we're at a standstill on a road hemmed in by tall pines.

"Thanks, Mom. Love you." Dad pulls out the earbuds, and I bite my lip to keep from peppering him with questions.

"Give me that clue."

His words send a jolt of excitement down to my toes. I dig through my pack for the notebook. We all hold our breath while he reads it, knowing how slim our chances of finding Uncle Elliot's treasure will be if he isn't on board.

"So…" Mom says softly, "What did she say?"

Dad scowls at the clue for a second longer. "She said he was a prisoner of war for two years and then stayed many years in Vietnam. He finally came back to the States but later returned numerous times to the country. After that, he was never in need of money. Aunt Amy told Mom that he's been planning this treasure hunt for years."

I suck in a long-needed breath. Dad looks at the map, checks the traffic in his mirror, and pulls into the left lane.

"You're right, Ruth. Northside Drive is not that far away."

"YES!" Sadie, Ethan, and I shout in unison.

-5-

I smoosh my cheek up against the cold window, trying to get a better view of the tunnel through the mountain we're about to enter. As the truck passes under the smooth arch, the light dims. The knowledge that the weight of a mountain now sits on top of us presses down on me. The tunnel lights flash by, making me think of the book of war stories I had started reading.

The tunnel seems to go on forever. Now the walls change from smooth concrete to roughhewn rock.

"Wow!" I whisper in awe. It's like I'm seeing the mountain's beating heart. Finally, the barest light of day shines ahead as we exit into the brilliant sunlight.

Mom gasps, and Sadie echoes her.

"What?" Ethan cranes his neck toward his window. "Is it a bear? I've got a really good bear joke."

But now I see what has captured their attention. I had read about Tunnel View, but no words could have prepared me for the sight of the huge granite mountains lining the long, forested valley. The river takes wing, diving over the sheer rock hundreds of feet high, shimmering like snow as it falls.

Without looking, I reach for Ethan's chin, but grab his nose instead.

"Hey!" he honks, his voice sounding funny as I use his nose to turn his head in the right direction. "Let go of my…"

But even he falls silent as he stares in awe at the view of Yosemite Valley that the photographer Ansel Adams had made famous. "Wow!" he echoes, and I grin at his nasal tone, finally letting go of his nose.

"It's like…" Mom's voice is gentle as she searches for the words but cannot find the right ones to describe the incredible beauty of the valley. We drive farther, still caught up in the awe of this incredible place.

When we finally turn onto Northside Drive, Dad's finger hits the window button. A blast of fresh air hits me. I breathe in the wild, clean scent and roll down my window too. Mom puts a hand over her mouth to cover a laugh. Northside Drive is filled with cars heading in both directions. In nearly every vehicle, people have their heads out the windows, shouting at the tops of their lungs.

"What say you? Shall we join them?" Dad asks with a grin.

Mom's laughter continues. She leans her head out of her window and lets out a rebel yell. I scramble forward, the wind buffeting my face.

"YYYYAAAAHHHHHH!"

Dad's shout puts the rest of ours to shame. I plug my ears and keep shouting as a boy in an oncoming car shouts out his window like me. Our eyes meet, our mouths wide open. I crumple back into a fit of laughter, plugging my ears tighter. Soon, tears are spilling down my cheeks, and I can hardly draw a breath. My laughter infects Sadie, then Ethan, then Mom and Dad. Finally, Dad wipes his face and says delightedly, "Well, that was quite an experience!"

Another carload of shouting people passes, and once again we all burst into giggles.

"Did we learn anything about the treasure?" Mom asks eventually.

"No!" Sadie says happily.

"Yes, we did!" Ethan insists. "It's incredibly *fun* to hunt for treasure."

As I roll up my window, a park ranger truck pulls to the side of the road. I notice the signs in the utility bed that look as if they've been hand-painted.

Ethan stretches to read them as we pass. "No shouting allowed."

"Well, it looks like we got here barely in time," Dad comments.

My nerves are tingling as we pull up at Curry Village. I can see the rows of straight-edged canvas tents. The brilliant white fabric reminds me of someone smiling. As Dad hops out of the truck, our feet hit the dirt at the same time. He looks over at me.

"$1 million in gold and gems…" I see a familiar glint in his eyes—the same one that shimmers when we're in a game of basketball, and he is playing to win.

That spark of enthusiasm, more than anything else, makes me believe that we are going to find Uncle Elliot's treasure. The thought thrills me down to my toes.

"Yes!" I pump my fist in the air.

His wide, strong hand grips my shoulder. "Let's get our stuff stowed in the tent and start hunting."

-6-

Firelight dances over Dad's face as he studies the clue. "It's an acrostic poem! We are in the right place!"

"What does *acrostic* mean?" Sadie leans closer.

"It's a poem where the first letter in each line spells out a new word. See here..." Dad points to the poem. "If you only take the first letter of each line you get the word..."

We all sound out the letters and excitedly say, "Yosemite! The treasure *is* here."

I bite my lower lip in excitement. As I look around the campfire in front of our canvas tent, all our eyes are bright, even Mom's.

"Um, Ethan…" Sadie cautions. "Your shish kebab is catching on fire."

"Ugh!" He yanks his stick from the fire, but the rush of air makes the flames flare on what once was veggies and meat. He desperately swings his stick from side to side in an effort to quench the flames, but he only succeeds in flinging his food off the end of the stick.

I duck and cover, as one chunk of seared zucchini strikes my shoulder. "I'm hit! I'm hit!"

"Ethan! Stop!" Mom jumps up and grabs Ethan's hand. He stares sadly at the charred remains of his dinner.

"Oh, man! I'm so hungry, and I almost had it just the way I like it."

While Mom prepares him another, I nibble mine and find it's just right.

"Ogle the pointy peaks that have never left." Dad is still deep in the clue as Sadie and I scoot closer so we can study the map on his lap with him.

"*Left* must be a direction, maybe standing for

west?" We let him think while Ethan starts roasting his dinner from scratch.

I look up at the incredible granite mountain faces framed by the shimmering stars. Yosemite looks like heaven to me. The way the trees yield to massive sheer rocks and the breathtaking waterfalls make me feel like we're on another planet. And somewhere, amidst all this beauty is a hidden treasure that I'm determined to find.

-7-

As I step out of our canvas tent, the sun is thinking about rising in the east. A light mist floats around my feet. The morning light is enough for me to find my way to the nearby restroom. A strong whiff of bacon makes my mouth water.

A few steps later, I can hear people talking. Without meaning to, I stop to listen. "That treasure's got to be between Half Dome and Clouds Rest," one voice declares.

"Great. We've narrowed it down to an area only 18.5 miles long." That voice drips with sarcasm.

A large Steller's Jay swoops past me, and its harsh cry makes me flinch. My face suddenly flushes. *I shouldn't have been listening.* But as I hurry along to our tent, I think about how easily I had overheard some campers' conversations. Clearly, the thin canvas does nothing to conceal voices. We will have to be extra careful to keep our communication about any clue extremely quiet.

I step back into our tent and ease back into my sleeping bag. Ethan and I sleep on the floor while Dad, Mom and Sadie have shared the large bed at one end of the tent.

My nose reawakens me the second time. Mom is toasting bread. Even before I open my eyes, a blast of wild cherry scent makes me smile. Ethan is already eating candy. Soon enough, our bellies are full, and we're huddled around the clue.

"I think we should head to Half Dome," Sadie says, pointing to the words *unsatisfied by half.*

"Shh, Sadie. The walls have ears. We've got to whisper."

Sadie looks at the walls, wide-eyed. "I don't see any ears."

"Isaiah is right; we should really keep quiet," Dad's voice is barely audible. So, we all move closer together and huddle.

"Half Dome is a 14-mile hike one way," Mom says softly.

"Besides," I add, "we don't *want* to be unsatisfied. I believe that line might be a warning *not* to go to Half Dome."

"Oh!" Sadie makes a shocked face.

"Today, we can either take the Mist Trail or the John Muir Trail," Dad says.

"Well, which one has the treasure on it?" Ethan whispers, slurring around his banana taffy.

"That's the million-dollar question," Dad says.

"Let's take the John Muir Trail today," Mom says confidently.

Dad nods. "All right, we pack for a full day out." I spin for my pack. *I'll need loads of water, trail food, and of course, the notebook.*

Curry Village is busy now in the rising heat of

midmorning. We sidestep groups of hikers who are studying maps, and soon we come to an open area. A man wearing the oddest contraption I've ever seen comes toward us. A small table with little slots containing pamphlets suspended from shoulder straps hangs near his stomach. He's wearing a multicolored cap with a little propeller on top as well. "Treasure maps!" he exclaims. "Get your treasure maps here!"

Dad holds up a hand as he approaches. "No, thank you."

We then come to a thin man standing on a rock. "Come on, folks! Only five dollars per recital of the clue! Audible learning will reveal what you've been missing. I have a trained theater voice that brings out secrets hiding within the details."

Someone steps up and hands the fellow money. He smiles and assumes a dramatic pose with his hands cupped around his mouth.

"Yell loudly on the drive; the north will be glad that you did."

"Yeah," Ethan adds, "but the park rangers won't!"

"Look at the pointy peaks that have never left." The man dramatically scans the horizon with one hand shielding his eyes from the sun.

Dad's nose wrinkles upward, and we all look confused. I pull out the old notebook, my finger landing on the word *ogle* instead of *look*.

"Enter the fog, only at the equinox will you draw closer."

I follow along as my family crowds around me, reading as well.

"At least he got that clue right," Ethan says.

"Go beyond the desire for silver snow, and go for the golden morning flair."

"Wrong again!" Sadie says in disgust.

"If you pass the curve, you'll reach the end, unsatisfied by half." The man's strong voice echoes in the trees.

"That one is right," I say.

"Turn aside from the common ground; Rick and Libby have done the same."

"Ummhumm," Ethan agrees after stuffing a blueberry taffy into his mouth.

"Tight in the cradle, 1001, though tiring are not fatal."

We all look at each other at his obvious error. The crowd that had gathered to listen breaks up without one word of complaint.

"Why didn't anybody else notice his mistakes?" Dad asks. I smile at the fire in his eyes. He's the smartest man I've ever known, and he's all in on this hunt.

The man calls for another five dollars. Dad steps up and slaps one into his palm. "Make sure you get every word right, will you?"

The man looks insulted. "My good sir, I assure you, you will never hear anything but perfection from me."

Dad simply crosses his arms over his muscular chest. I do the same, wishing I had lifted more weights last winter.

A crowd bunches around us to listen, but once

again, the man repeats his mistakes this time through as well.

"You're saying it wrong!" Ethan cries when the man is finished. "It should be o...!"

Dad's wide hand clamps over Ethan's mouth. He smiles tightly at the man, then Dad's expression changes to disgust. As he removes his hand from Ethan's mouth, a long string of sticky taffy stretches between them.

"Oh, gross!" Mom says, digging in her pack for a wipe.

"But Uncle Greg..." Ethan starts to protest, sucking the taffy back into his mouth.

"Yes, Ethan, something's going on here, but let's keep it to ourselves. Okay?" Dad says softly as he cleans his hands.

"Maps! Get your treasure maps!" The man with the propeller hat strides by again.

"Sir! We'll take one after all," Dad says, choosing the largest printout.

"Come on!" Dad steps off the trail, and we follow

him into the trees. I can barely stand the wait. Finally, he stops and flattens out the clue.

Sure enough, it reads exactly the way the man had recited it. *Wrong in three spots!*

"Wait a minute!" Sadie cries. "Which one is right? Ours or theirs?"

But Dad is squinting, thinking hard. "Let me see the notebook."

I hand it to him, my fingers tingling. He studies the two side-by-side for so long I think I might burst.

"Maybe neither one is wrong," he says.

"How can that be?" Mom's voice holds a tinge of exasperation.

"Uncle Elliot only changed three words, but they were very strategic changes."

"How so?" Ethan asks, scowling at the papers.

"Remember how I said that ours is an acrostic poem? The first letter of each line spells a word. Well, the new clues don't. Now the acrostic spells *YLEGITT.*"

Sadie giggles as Dad sounds it out.

"Well, one of them must be wrong," Mom insists.

"Maybe he didn't want to give away the park name, so he changed it. We'll simply have to work from both clues and make sure our solutions work for both."

A grin steals across my face. "In other words, we've got insider information!"

Dad nods. "We're probably the only people other than Uncle Elliot who *know* the treasure is in Yosemite National Park."

- 8 -

I place the map and notebook next to each other. Mom is getting lunch together, and we've got to choose which way to search today.

"Ogle the pointy peaks," I mutter the words for the hundredth time as I run my finger over the map of Yosemite.

"Hey, Isaiah," Ethan calls. "My brother told me the treasure was buried in a well."

"Ethan, you don't have a brother; you're an only child."

"Oh, come on, play along."

"Fine. Why did your nonexistent brother tell you that?"

"Because I fell for it!" He cackles with laughter at his own joke, and I shake my head.

"That wasn't even funny," I say, turning back to the map. I stare at my finger; it's pointing to a mountain called Grizzly Peak.

"Peak?" I scowl at the map. *Is this location part of the clue?* My breath catches in my throat.

"DAD!" I shout, making Ethan spin my way in a ninja pose. Dad steps into the canvas tent with Sadie right on his heels.

"I love you more," he says to her.

"No, Dad!" she declares happily, "I love you more." They've been playing this game for quite a while, and I'm not sure who's winning.

"Look at this!" My finger taps the map of its own accord. "Peak and point!"

"So what?" Sadie says.

"Look, there's Grizzly Peak and right next to it is Sierra Point! *Pointy peaks!*"

Dad's focus is intent as he leans in closer. "I think you're onto something here, Isaiah." I bite my lip in excitement. *"Ogle the pointy peaks that have never left."*

"Hey! Maybe the clue doesn't mean the mountains haven't left. What if it is a direction like to keep Sierra Point and Grizzly Peak on our left!" Sadie whispers.

"Yes!" I pound my finger onto the map with excitement. "If we keep them to the left, we would be on the…Mist Trail!"

"Mmmm," Dad murmurs. "That's the same trail that eventually leads to Half Dome. Well, Rawlings family, I think we have our second clue figured out. Entering the park on Northside Drive leads to the Mist Trailhead."

"Let's go!" I say, but then I freeze as I hear something brush against the tent.

"What was that?" Ethan asks.

I rush out of the tent and catch sight of a tall boy running away. I grit my teeth. *I'm sure he overheard our plans.*

"Turns out..." Ethan pants with one hand over his chest. "The Mist Trail is uphill both ways."

I gulp some water, but the treasure pulls me forward. One thing is clear: thousands of other people are also searching for Uncle Elliot's treasure. We press forward, passing massive granite boulders and some of the biggest trees I've ever seen. All around us, I see people everywhere studying the clues.

We squeeze onto a crowded wooden bridge suspended over an incredible, bluish-colored creek crashing through enormous stones. I can't help hearing the whispered words of a couple standing on the bridge. "*Silver snow* must refer to the Silver Apron," the couple says as they point to their map.

I bite my lip and pull out my map as we hike off the bridge. Sure enough, far ahead on the Mist Trail is a place called *Silver Apron*. My heart pounds… but not from the elevation gain.

"Uncle Greg," Ethan says, pointing farther into the woods. "Is that what I think it is?"

I peer through the trees. Something is flying through the air with rhythmic timing.

Dad squints. "I'm pretty sure that digging in a national park is forbidden."

Now I can see a man with a shovel, flinging dirt high over one shoulder.

"If that's true, then how will we find it?" Ethan stops short, and Sadie plows into his pack.

"Ethan!" She rubs her nose. "You need brake lights!"

"Well, I don't think it *is* buried," says Dad quietly.

I flinch at Dad's quiet words. "What?"

"Think about it. If Uncle Elliot buried it in a national park, then he already broke the rules. From everything I've heard about my uncle, he would've obeyed the rules."

"Dad!" I hissed, "Shh." People are staring at Dad as if he's grown wings or sprouted horns.

Dad looks around, noticing. He offers a tight smile, raising his voice. "Yeah, *Uncle* Elliot. That's what everybody calls him, right?"

I watch the other hunters closely, but most of them are looking suspiciously at Dad. We picked up the pace to a jog up a steep section, putting some distance between us and everyone who had heard Dad.

At the top of the hill, a ravine opens to the right, and I see thick woods with cliffs on either side. Ethan is hauling in air so hard that his face is as red as a beet.

"Let's take a break," Mom gasps, stepping off the path and sitting down.

Two boys step out from the shadows of the trees, each holding a stout branch.

"Am I seeing double?" Ethan whispers to Sadie and me.

"I know *I* am," Sadie responds. The tall boys with thick brown hair, bright-blue eyes, and identical faces are exact replicas of each other.

"Oh, hello," Mom says.

The boy on her left merely scowls, but the other nods at us uncertainly. He appears to want to say something but thinks better of it.

"Excuse me, but what exactly are your intentions with that stick?" Ethan asks boldly.

The boy on Mom's left smacks the branch ominously on his palm, but the other shrinks back a bit, his eyes dropping to the forest floor.

Dad stations himself between us and the twins as Mom passes out some food. Sadie takes a handful of beef jerky and walks toward the boy on Mom's right.

"Hi. I'm Sadie. Would you like some?"

He's nearly Ethan's height—far taller than she is, and his eyes flick to hers in surprise.

"Oh, um, thanks." He takes some and smiles shyly at her.

"Brody!" the other boy snarls in a scolding voice.

Dad and I watch him closely. *I don't trust him with that stick he's holding.*

Brody shrinks back a little more as Sadie offers his brother some. The other boy doesn't respond; he simply smacks the branch in his palm again.

Sadie shrugs, putting a piece in her mouth.

"Okay…" Mom says, clearly uncomfortable. "I think we should keep moving."

"See you, Brody," Sadie says with a bright smile and a wave.

"Yeah, see you," Brody replies, a sheepish smile on his face. His brother takes a menacing step toward his brother, who looks back toward the ground.

We head back to the path, but Ethan grabs my elbow. "Look!"

His excited whisper makes me turn. A tall man strides from the woods, snapping his fingers at the boys. They jump to attention, and Brody takes a folding shovel from him.

"That's the man with the limp from the plane!" Sadie says for our ears alone.

What feels like a streak of electricity races across my chest. I don't doubt my inner warning system. That feeling is never wrong. *This man is dangerous.*

I guide Sadie forward, away from him.

"You like Brody, don't you?" Ethan's voice drips with a singsong, teasing tone.

"Not like that. He seems so sad; I don't like to see people feel that way."

I hadn't really thought of his demeanor as sad, but now I know she's right.

"I don't trust their dad or his brother though—not even a little," I add.

- 10 -

"Wait a minute," Dad says, staring up at a high, beautiful falls. As the water dives off the sheer granite cliff, the droplets seem to disintegrate at the bottom into a thick mist.

"I'll wait five," Ethan says, holding his side. The last stone staircase to reach the falls had been tough.

"This is *Vernal Falls*," Dad adds. I can see he's thinking hard, and my excitement rises.

"So?"

When Dad looks around at the crowd suspiciously, I *know* he's figured out something else.

"Come on. Let's find a quiet place." I bite my lip, desperate to know what he does.

"Here, we can slip past these rocks."

I hurry forward, turning sideways to squeeze between the boulders. I can't wait for Mom, the last of our group to join us. "What? Did you figure it out?"

Sadie is clinging to Dad's muscular arm. "What?"

He can't hide a wide grin. "We're on the right path!"

My stomach does a flip. Ethan had just stuffed a cherry taffy into his mouth, "Fffttt…MMMMM!"

"Yes, Ethan." Dad says, hands on his hip, with a satisfied grin spreading across his face. "We're at *Vernal* Falls. Twice a year, an event happens called an equinox which occurs when the position of the sun is exactly over the equator. One is called the autumnal equinox; the other is the *vernal* equinox. At this time, the hours of daylight and the hours of darkness are about equal almost everywhere on earth."

"*Enter the fog, only at the equinox, will you draw closer!*" Sadie cries.

"Yes, we are drawing closer."

"Wait," Mom says. "Wasn't there another clue before that one?"

"Yes, and I think we've just gotten that one too. *Somewhere below lies one silhouette of George, white-haired and ancient.*" Dad pulls out his map. With our heads together, I hold my breath as he traces the Mist Trail past Grizzly Peak and Sierra Point.

"Wait!" Ethan blasts us with a strong cherry scent. "Illilouette Gorge!"

"*Exactly!* Just south of Grizzly Peak is Illilouette Gorge, home to another waterfall. Did you notice how the Vernal Falls looked like long white hair before it hits the rocks?"

"And it certainly is ancient!" My fingers are tingling. *We could find it today!*

"Whashhh de nix clooo?" Ethan slurs, his jaws practically glued together by a watermelon taffy.

"*Move beyond the desire for silver snow and go for the golden morning flare.*" *Leave it to Dad to have the entire acrostic memorized.*

"What on earth could that mean?" Sadie has her hands on her cheeks.

"Mmmm fla." Ethan swallows the taffy practically whole. "*Morning flare*—maybe it can only be seen if there's lightning in the morning?"

"*Silver snow*," Mom mutters as we step back onto the trail.

"I overheard some other hikers. They thought silver snow meant the Silver Apron."

"That would fit exactly!" Dad says excitedly.

"Oh, no," I say, catching sight of Brody. He's weighed down by a huge pack while his brother and Dad carry nothing on their backs as they look at what must be a copy of the clue. A large group has gathered, looking at the falls.

"Hey!" an excited voice calls. "Look! It's Elliot Elkland!"

I spin around, searching for his face.

"Yeah!" another person calls, "It's him!"

"Oh, no," Mom says as people begin pointing toward us.

"Do they mean Dad?" Sadie whispers, her eyes growing wide.

"I'm afraid so."

"Who are they pointing at?" Dad asks Mom under his breath.

"You, honey."

Dad remains quiet for a moment while the shouting increases. "This...could be bad."

"Yeah, for sure."

"Give us a clue, Elliot!" one man in the crowd shouts. Dad shakes his head in dismay, but more people take up the line until it becomes a chant among many.

"Give us a clue! Give us a clue!"

"I'm not Elliot Elkland!" Dad shouts, but clearly no one believes him. My skin crawls as the man from the plane shoves his way through the mob. Sweat beads on my upper lip.

"Listen!" Dad has his hands spread in front of him. "My name is Greg...Greg Rawlings!"

"Give us a clue!"

The mass of people is pressing closer, making my chest ache.

"Greg, what are we going to do?" Mom's voice is tight as we face down the crowd.

"Here, I'll prove it to you!" Dad pulls his wallet from his back pocket, taking out his work identification card with his photo and name printed on it. "See? Greg Rawlings!"

The gathering is pressed against us now. One man squints at the card, then at Dad.

"I say the card is a fake! Give us a clue, Elliot! Or better yet, take us to the treasure!"

Mom grips one of Sadie's elbows and one of mine in her hands. My heart slams against my ribs. All the faces in the crowd are growing more menacing by the moment.

"Grrreeggg!" Mom shrieks in fear.

I've never heard Mom's voice sound like that.

"Check him for the tattoo!"

"Yeah, that tattoo will tell us who he is!"

Dad swallows hard. "What tattoo?" he says to

the crowd. Then he turns to Mom. "I surely hope this tattoo isn't in some *embarrassing* place."

Four men step forward, and Dad crouches, his eyes darting between them. My mouth is suddenly so dry I can't swallow. A man snatches Dad's wrist, and a struggle results as the other three grasp his other arm. I want to shout at them to stop, but I'm frozen to the spot. Sadie gasps, tears in her eyes as Dad tenses.

He's a good wrestler. I've tested him out plenty of times, and I know he could easily take at least two at a time, but the entire mob leans forward as the first man lifts Dad's forearm with a frown.

"No tattoo…"

The disappointed crowd sighs, and everyone grumbles. The men release Dad, and I breathe for the first time since they grabbed him.

Sadie rushes forward to Dad, hugging him hard as he scowls at the dispersing crowd. With a shock I realize the man from the plane is still glaring at Dad, his arms crossed as he studies Dad's face.

"No, no, no," I whisper. Dad glares right back until Brody's dad turns away.

"Uncle Greg, I think you should wear my hat," Ethan suggests. His face is white as he hands it over, his hair sticking up at odd angles. Dad adjusts the size and puts it on.

"I don't think that's quite enough," Mom adds, pulling her favorite pair of sunglasses from her pack. Dad looks at the feminine black glasses and shakes his head.

"Dad, those people would have done whatever they wanted to you," I say, one hand against my chest.

"That was really scary!" Sadie adds. She is still hugging Dad.

"Okay. I'll put them on. I wonder what kind of tattoo...*Mr.* Elkland has?"

- 11 -

It's nearly dark by the time we trudge back to Curry Village. The brilliant white canvas fabric of the tents takes on the colors of sunset. We pass a family gathered around a campfire. The scent of their hamburgers grilling over the coals makes my stomach growl.

"Hello!" a heavyset man calls to us as he flips the sizzling meat. "You all out here hunting treasure?" We look at each other suspiciously. "I'm Dave, and all hunters are welcome at my fire." Dave's hazel eyes peer over his plump red cheeks, and his wild beard moves as he speaks.

Somehow, I know we can trust him.

"You look hungry. We've got enough to feed an army! Why don't you join us?" Dave shifts, reaching toward the campfire to flip the farthest burger.

"That..." Dad says, "sounds great."

"I'll bring over some side dishes," Mom adds.

Dave chuckles and says, "I don't look like I would refuse food, do I?"

For the first time all day, I feel at ease around someone other than my family.

"I'm Reuben," says a boy who's a smaller version of his dad. He looks like he's about nine years old. By the time we're all gathered around the fire, all I can think about is the food.

"Juicy burgers...come to Papa!" Ethan states.

"Now, there is a man after my own heart!" Dave slaps Ethan on the back. "Here, have the first one."

"No pickles for Ethan, please!" Mom says. I grin, as I remember what had happened to him when we visited the Grand Tetons.

"Ah, in that case, you can have the second one!" Dave hands the first burger to me. It might be the best thing I have ever put into my mouth, complete with the flavor of campfire and pickles.

For a while, we're all silent, gobbling the food as the damp coolness of night coats us and the stars appear above.

"You know, this treasure hunt has changed our lives," Dave says, wiping ketchup from his beard with his forearm.

Ethan chokes on his last bite. I slap him vigorously on his back until he gets a clear breath.

"You found it?" he squeaks, his eyes watering.

Dave throws back his head with a hearty laugh, "NO! But you know, about a month ago, all we did was sit at the house and watch TV." Dave looks up at the inky black sky glittering with stars. "I'd forgotten how beautiful and how exciting the world is. These last two weeks my family has hiked 15 miles, lost 25 pounds between all of us, and *experienced* life. I've also gotten to know my kids better, for real. We've talked about things—deep things that really matter."

Dave's white teeth shine through his thick beard. "So, really, Elliot Elkland gave us a fresh shot at life."

"I guess that's a treasure in and of itself," Dad says softly.

"Worth far more than a million." The warmth around the fire is deeper than I've ever felt. Dave and his family are *happy.* They are the direct opposite to most of the other hunters.

"I keep hearing about a tattoo that Mr. Elkland has. You wouldn't happen to know what it looks like, do you?" Dad asks.

Dave holds up his forearm and rolls up his sleeve. On his wrist, I can just make out a black mark. "Sure can. It looks just like this one…well, pretty near anyway. I did mine with a permanent marker."

Ethan leans in closer. "Why would someone have a bunch of numbers tattooed on his wrist?"

"Well, young man…" Dave's meaty hand grips Ethan's thin shoulder. "There is actually quite a story behind it. During the Vietnam War, soldiers taken captive were sometimes tattooed with their prisoner number. It wasn't too common, but Mr. Elkland received one—97265—while serving our country."

We all fall silent, staring at the numbers on Dave's wrist. I try to imagine being taken captive, like I've been reading about in the war stories, and I wonder if I'd have the courage to face the unknown.

"I'm honored to wear the numbers for a while," Dave says wistfully. "And I wish I could thank Mr. Elkland for his service to this country and all he's done for my family."

We all stare at the numbers—especially how the marker had kind of bled into his skin so that the edges are blurred.

"You know, Greg, you look a lot like him," Dave says as he studies Dad.

"Trust me, I have been hearing that," Dad responds softly. "Dave, joining you at your fire tonight has been a great ending to our day."

We say goodnight then make our way quietly to the canvas tent.

-12-

The second my eyes pop open, all I want to do is run for the Silver Apron and decode the rest of the clue. Apparently, Dad feels the same way.

"Come on, let's get Ethan up."

I roll over and shake Ethan's shoulder. At least I think it's his shoulder. He's got the hood of his sleeping bag closed off so tight he looks like a giant sausage.

"Ethan," I hiss. No response. *Maybe he didn't get enough air in there.* Worried now, I shake him harder. Still nothing. Dad and I look at each other.

Dad's strong hands move Ethan's entire sleeping bag. We hear a snort and some mumbling from inside. "Twenty, no! I'll take forty duplex cookies, please."

I cover a laugh of relief, but Ethan grows still as stone as soon as Dad stops shaking him.

"I got this, Dad. Go ahead and stoke the fire," I whisper. Eventually, I resort to pouncing on Ethan.

"Don't take the Twizzlers! Those are mine!" He groans.

"Ethan!" He starts to twist, and I feel like I am wrestling an octopus. "It's time to find the treasure!" I whisper harshly. He flinches under me.

"Treasure?" I finally hear his real awake voice.

"Hurry up!"

By the time we're back at the Silver Apron, it's not even 10:00 a.m. I have a good feeling about today. The air above the rushing water feels charged with excitement. Here, the river spreads out over a gently arched piece of granite, and the water ripples, looking only a few inches deep.

"Today's the day! I know it." Ethan has his map upside down.

"Ethan, you're holding it wrong," Sadie says.

"No, sometimes when you look at things from a different angle, you see something new."

I try to figure out which compass direction on his map is pointing at me. *It must be…east—the direction the sun rises.*

"Remember the sunrises in Grand Teton?" I say to no one in particular.

"Oh, yeah," Ethan says, "I remember intensely studying the insides of my eyelids during those."

I roll my eyes at his reply. I had been busy starting the campfire before the sun rose with its intense colors flaring in all directions. I grip Ethan's forearm, my knuckles white. He strikes another ninja pose, searching for an enemy. "What is it, a grizzly?"

"A grizzly hasn't been seen in Yosemite since 1920," Sadie says. "All the bears here are American black bears, though they may have brown fur."

"So is it a black or a brown American black bear?" he asks, leaping about and scanning the trail.

"No, it's east! You were right, Ethan. Looking at the map cockeyed really did work!"

"Slow down and explain yourself," Sadie orders.

"Open the clue! *Go for the golden flare!* That means *sunrise!* Where does the sun come up? In the east. We need to cross the Merced River to be on the east side of Silver Apron!"

Sadie snatches the map from Ethan. "Look! Right ahead is a footbridge to do exactly that!"

Dad strides up and studies his map. "You might just be on to something there, kids," he says.

-13-

We've hiked over the wooden footbridge, and I have to work at slowing my pace. *We are so close! Only three clues to go.*

Mom wants something out of her pack, and I have to bite my tongue to keep from complaining about the holdup.

Sadie, Ethan, and I sit cross-legged near the trail with a map spread in front of us.

"So, we're here." Ethan points to the Mist Trail.

"Um…no, we're not." Sadie scowls.

"Sure, we are," Ethan disagrees, popping a watermelon taffy into his mouth.

"I'll take one," Sadie says easily.

Ethan scowls at the map as he pulls one from his pack.

"No!" I shout, catapulting over the map. I slap the taffy out of his hand, and Sadie makes a grab for it.

"Ethan, what are you thinking?"

Sadie scrambles for the candy, but my hand closes around it before hers. Ethan ignores my comment as he pulls the now crumpled map from beneath me.

"We are right here." He points to a spot far ahead of where we are on the trail.

"Sadie's right; we're right here at this curve." My head snaps up, and so do Sadie's and Ethan's.

"If you pass the curve, you'll reach the end, unsatisfied by half."

We lean over the map, our heads pressed together. "If we went straight after the footbridge…" Ethan traces the path with one finger.

"We'd be headed due east!" Sadie exclaims. My breath comes faster. *Only two clues to go!*

"Dad!" I turn to rush toward him, but he's already striding our way. "We went too far!" we say in unison, trying to keep our voices low.

"I know."

I laugh. *Of course, Dad would've thought of that!*

"Come on, troops! Let's get back and head east."

We rushed back to the footbridge, only to find a large crowd gathered there. Conversations fall silent as we pass groups staring at us suspiciously. All the people here are studying maps and the clues. Suddenly, not giving away our solution seems impossible.

"How do we head east without…you know…" Ethan whispers, eyeing the crowd.

Dad scans our surroundings. "I say we take a break right over here," he declares loudly. He's still wearing Ethan's hat and Mom's glasses. None of us want a repeat of last time. We follow Dad a few steps into the dense pine forest and settle down for a snack that I don't want to eat. Ethan snatches the uneaten trail mix from my hand.

Yosemite Fortune

"Thanks," he says, stuffing it in his mouth.

"Here's the plan." Dad keeps his voice low, "Ruth, you take Sadie off into the woods. That will look like nothing more than a bathroom break. Then, one at a time, Isaiah and Ethan, you head over to those boulders. From there, stay out of sight and wait for me by the mouth of the canyon. We'll all meet there." He barely nods to the east where the feet of two mountains nearly touch.

Mom tightens her pack with a glint of determination in her eyes. I cover a grin as I realize the thought of the treasure has gripped even her.

She and Sadie wander into the woods. It seems like a month passes before Dad imperceptibly nods at me. I scan the milling crowds near the bridge. Only a few people are looking our way. I wait a moment longer, wishing I were wearing camouflage clothing. I try not to hurry as sweat breaks out between my shoulder blades.

I find an easy path that winds behind a pile of massive stones. The air is perfectly still, and my own breath sounds too loud. I run a hand over the cold stone, looking way up at the granite face of the mountain. And for the merest moment, I'm a part of this incredible place that looks like heaven and smells like it too.

"Ouch!"

I jerk around at the intrusion. *Ethan*. He's sucking on his finger as he strides up to me. "Watch out for the thorns. I wonder if Uncle Elliot put the treasure in a bramble bush?"

As quickly as the intense peace comes, it disintegrates. All the pressure of finding the treasure hits me full force.

I glimpse a bit of blue cloth as I sidestep a vine. *It must be Mom and Sadie.*

"Ouch! Ethan exclaims, catching his leg and its thorny embrace.

"Shh! We are supposed to be sneaking."

"Right, ow!"

Soon, we're with Mom and Sadie at the mouth of what looks like a very narrow canyon.

"Where is Dad?" I crane my neck but don't catch a glimpse of him.

Mom wrings her hands together. "I'm not sure. Maybe I should go check." I know she is thinking of the mob's insisting Dad was Uncle Elliot.

"Will you be all right for a few moments?" she asks, still searching the way we came.

"Sure, Mom," I say. "Can we hike some in this little canyon?"

She glances that way. "Okay, but not very far."

"Sure, Aunt Ruth. I will take good care of them," Ethan promises.

That response gives Mom a pause, and she looks ready to take back her words.

"We'll be fine, Mom," Sadie insists.

Soon we're hiking between sheer granite cliffs. This canyon is so narrow that I can see both sides at the same time.

Ethan snaps a branch, and I swallow hard. Suddenly, I'm fighting a tingling sensation in my chest.

"Wait a minute," I say softly, one arm catching

Sadie's pack and forcing her to a halt. Ethan stuffs a blueberry taffy into his mouth, turning to look at me. "Wash?"

"Wash what?" Sadie asks, screwing up one side of her nose.

He shakes his head, his lips turning blue from the candy. "Whhhaasshhh?"

His jaws must be glued together.

"Quiet! Something's not right," I say.

Sadie looks at me sharply, but the sensation only grows, so I don't let go of her pack. Sadie and I freeze at a whisper of sound. Ethan can't hear it as he smacks his lips.

-14-

"There!" Sadie whispers, pointing beyond Ethan. I don't see anything, but my nerves are so keyed up I can barely stand still.

Ethan is still oblivious to what is happening, as he digs at his molars with one finger.

A shout rends the air, and I crouch, searching for the source of the roar. My hair stands on end as I spot something leaping toward Ethan!

His eyes bug out, his legs stretch out to run, but they go nowhere as his feet slip on the wet leaves. He can barely scream with his mouth glued shut by taffy. Blue drool drips down his chin.

"Rrrrrraaaahhhh!"

Now I can make out a form of some kind about Ethan's height that stops behind him.

Sadie clamps one hand over her chest, sagging with relief. "It's just a boy!"

I'm not so sure. The figure seems like a fragment of the forest itself with twigs and grass stuck all over it.

Ethan's desperate legs finally gain some traction, and he zooms past us.

"Ethan, stop!" Sadie calls, her tension giving way to laughter. The figure makes another movement, and now I can see what Sadie meant. What I am seeing is a tall boy whose face has been painted like tree bark. He is covered from head to toe in a suit that has a ragged forest fabric sticking out all over it. Another boy then steps from hiding, and my stomach hits my toes.

"Oh," I say, stepping in front of Sadie.

Grinning, she leans around me. "Hey, Brody!" she says easily to the second boy who had appeared.

"Get out of here!" the first boy says with a sinister gleam in his eyes.

"The woods don't belong to you," I retort before thinking.

"They do now. Try getting past here, and I'll teach you how much I own the woods."

"Brock," Brody says softly, shaking his head. He looks as embarrassed as a boy who's dressed in full camouflage can be.

I don't take my eyes off Brock—not with that warning pulsing strongly in my chest.

"Be quiet, Brody! Dad told us to guard this valley, so you'd better do your part," Brock snarls.

Brody shifts from one foot to the other, his eyes on the ground. At least I think they are; the face paint makes it super hard to tell.

Sadie smiles sadly at Brody, and my frustration brings more words. "This is public land; you can't keep us off of it."

"I keep *all* enemies off *my* land."

"I'm not your enemy, and this land is not your

land! This land is public land." I wish my voice didn't sound so stressed.

"Oh, yes, you are! You and every other treasure hunter in Yosemite are my enemies. If you come any farther, you won't even be safe in your fancy little white tent." A shiver of dread runs down my spine. *He knows where we sleep!* My muscles clench as I sense motion behind us.

"Woohoo!" Ethan says. "I thought it was a bear."

"I'm worse," Brock says.

Ethan leans forward, squinting. "The question is, what are you?" I know he's joking, but his question doesn't go over well with Brock.

"I'm your worst nightmare."

"Oh, no. You're definitely wrong there. My worst nightmare involved a 40-pound hotdog slathered in ketchup, mustard, and relish as it chased me down the road."

I glance at Ethan, wide-eyed. A chuckle escapes Brody, and soon he, Sadie and I are all laughing out loud.

"Hey, that nightmare was no laughing matter! I couldn't sleep for days," Ethan adds.

"Brody!" Brock snaps, making Brody stand at attention. "I'll tell Dad if you keep this up. And you don't want that to happen. Now, the rest of you, get out of here."

"I don't like your tone of voice, young man," Ethan says, jutting out his scrawny chest.

Brock takes a menacing step forward.

This is bad.

"And I don't like *you*," Brock snarls.

"Where do you get off being so rude? You owe me an apology," Ethan says, stalking toward Brock.

"Never!" Brock lowers his head.

This is really bad. Only two strides are left between them.

"I say we end this right here. You against me. When I win, you leave," Brock declares.

Brody's mouth is hanging open in horror, so I know Brock isn't bluffing the way Ethan is.

"*When* you win? Au contraire, sir!"

They're nose to nose now, and Ethan looks decidedly less threatening with blue taffy spit still stuck to his chin.

"Isaiah, do something!" Sadie whispers, gripping my arm. But I have no idea how to break the building tension. They lean closer yet.

"BOYS!" A deep voice reverberates between the tight mountains, and I'm filled with relief as they step apart.

Sadie leans on my arm as Dad strides between Ethan and Brock.

"Whatever you two have going on, you'd better cool it." Dad's voice has a note of steel I've never heard, and his muscles strain at his shirt. Brock drops his gaze, but his jaw is still clenched tight.

"Rawlings kids, we're heading out."

"Bu…" Ethan starts, then snaps his mouth shut. "Yes, sir."

Sadie smiles and waves at Brody, who once again looks embarrassed to have any connection to his twin brother.

Yosemite Fortune

We hike back to the Merced River, and Dad turns to us. "What on earth was that all about?"

Ethan and I keep our eyes glued to the ground.

"Brock said he owned the valley and that we couldn't pass," Sadie explains. "Ethan, you've got blue taffy all over your chin."

"I do?" His hand goes to his face. "How embarrassing! Why didn't you tell me?"

Before Sadie can respond, Dad heaves a heavy sigh. "It's just as I thought."

My eyes go wide as Dad turns to scan the distant canyon entrance, rubbing his stubbled face.

"What are you thinking?" I ask.

"*Turn aside from the common ground* means leave the trail. *Rick and Libby have done the same.*"

"Is that supposed to be some sort of explanation?"

He hands me the map. Determined to figure it out, I study the glossy paper in the fading light. Dad already told us the answer to the first half of this line. *Rick and Libby have done the same...* My finger lands on the small area between the Merced River and Liberty Cap. *Really, there's not much here.* The sheer mountains would soon trap us on one side, and the Silver Apron on the other. *Wait, a minute!*

"*Liberty...Libby?* Could *liberty* be the Libby he's talking about?" I cry.

"Shh," Dad warns.

Sadie and Ethan rush over with a gasp. Sadie points to the other mountain that makes up the far wall of the valley the twins are guarding. "Mount Broderick! That's Rick!"

"Precisely," Dad agrees. "Except we are not the first people to figure it out."

- 15 -

Scouting the area below Liberty Cap and Mount Broderick only confirms the one entrance and one "cradle."

"Only 1001 steps away!" Ethan whines as we consider the fading sun. We've got miles to get back to our rather unsafe-from-Brock tent before dark.

We end up back near the footbridge, nervous that Brody and Brock will find the treasure first. Mom insists that we start back to camp, but I would do about anything to stay right here! A ranger hikes across the bridge and raises a bullhorn to her mouth.

"Hikers, attention please. The Mono Lake fire

has spread far faster than the worst of our predictions. You can see the smoke now." The entire crowd turns to look at the ominous black smudge hanging over Mount Broderick. "All hikers must return to Yosemite Valley immediately."

"I thought it was getting dark earlier than normal." Ethan pounds his fist into his palm. "We're so close!"

"Shh!" I hiss as people turn to look at Ethan. *We won't be able to persuade Mom to stay out here now.*

As we trudge heavily over the bridge, Ethan veers off toward the ranger. "Excuse me, ma'am?" He points to the map in his hand. "Three more hikers are right here in this valley. Two of them are in camouflage, but you'd better get them out. I think they're planning to stay the night."

"Thank you very much for this report, young man. There's no camping in Yosemite without a permit, so they definitely won't be staying."

I breathe a quiet sigh of relief.

-16-

The sharp scent of acrid smoke is curling into my nostrils. By the time we get back to Curry Village, we are using our flashlights.

"What on earth?" Ethan says, shining his light at the ground. A man is lying flat on the dirt beside a canvas tent. Even stranger is the fact that he's weeping…and not quietly as huge sobs shake his body.

"Greg," Mom says, looking toward an entire group of people farther ahead who are in nearly the same condition. "This is making me nervous. Has some sort of disaster taken place? Is this because of the fire?"

A hearty laugh echoes, and I recognize Dave's voice. "A disaster of sorts anyway! The treasure of Elliot Elkland has been found!"

I feel as if someone has punched me in the gut, leaving me gasping for air like a fish out of water.

"Noooo!" Ethan wails, his fists clenched as he falls to his knees.

Emotions including jealousy, anger, and regret pummel me. They flow so fast that my stomach sours.

"Brock and Brody found it! Arghh!" I spin toward a nearby tree and barely keep myself from punching it. A broken hand wouldn't help anything, but I'm overwhelmed by the crushing sense of loss.

"Come on and sit for a while. We've got red hots on the fire tonight." Dave's soothing voice draws us closer. My family's faces are as stunned as mine. We are all trying to assimilate the fact that we've failed.

"There's no point in missing a meal over it,"

Dave adds, "not with all the exercise we've gotten today. Right, Rudy?"

"Yeah, besides, we've already got our treasure!"

"You do?" Ethan's voice cracks pitifully on the last word.

Rudy hugs Dave. "Yep, it's our family!"

I swallow hard, but I can't eat the hot dog that Dave hands to me.

We call it a night early and trudge down the lane to our bright, white tent.

Dad shrugs off his pack, "I *really* thought we would be the ones to find it. I guess because Elliot is my uncle."

I can't even formulate words as I numbly lie on my sleeping bag. Eventually the hard ground forces me to roll, but no matter how I try, I can't fall asleep—not with the greatest failure of my life smashing me. And then too, Uncle Elliot's compass is still stuck in my pocket, and it's pressed against my skin.

-17-

A wide-shouldered shadow is passing outside. Disoriented in the dark, I whisper, "Dad?" *He must be heading to the bathrooms.* I scramble up to follow him, trying to escape the strangeness of the dream I'd been having. We'd been trying to catch a golden fish that was flopping on shore, but none of us could hold onto our slippery catch.

"Dad!" I whisper into the sharp coolness of night. He doesn't turn toward my voice, so I jog forward toward him. His muscular shoulders give him that familiar wedge shape.

"Wait up, Dad," I pant the words as loud as I dare as we pass through the rows of tents.

Still, he keeps on walking. I'm only two steps behind him now, and we pass under a security light. *Odd...he's still wearing Ethan's hat this late?* But then something else catches my attention. My eyes narrow. *When did Dad put a fake tattoo on his wrist? That's not something he would do.*

Biting my lip, I change my walk into a creep, suddenly trying to keep quiet and wondering why Dad hadn't responded to me. In a few more steps we pass under another light, and I stifle a gasp. The stubble of Dad's beard is gray! My heart starts to pound. *Is this still a dream? If so, it's the weirdest one yet.*

He reaches up to rub his neck, and my mouth falls open. *The numbers on his wrist are clear as can be. That's no mere marker!*

"Um... Am..." My voice is a jumble. *What do I do? Do I let him walk away? Is this really Uncle Elliot? I've got to know!*

"Um...Uncle Elliot?" My voice finally obeys me. The man stops, and I freeze, my eyes wide.

Slowly, he turns, and I nearly laugh at the huge pair of black sunglasses he's wearing; they're just like Dad's…well, Mom's.

"Uncle Elliot?" I whisper, staring up at him.

"Go on, kid. I'm not your uncle." His voice is even similar to Dad's! He turns to go.

"Sure, you are!" I rush ahead, desperate to make him stop. "Your nephew, Greg Rawlings, is my dad. So that makes you my uncle…I think. Great-uncle, maybe?"

He narrows his eyes. "I haven't heard that name in years. That's a clever story, kid, but I don't believe you." Uncle Elliot strides on, making me wonder how many people have shown up at his door, claiming to be his blood kin since he'd hidden the treasure.

"Wait! I can prove it!" I leapfrog him again and desperately yank at the heavy brass compass in my pocket. I growl at it as he sidesteps me. *The crazy thing is jammed in my pocket worse than ever!*

"Uncle Elliot, wait!" I rip desperately at my stubborn pocket. *He's getting away!* If he passes into the deep dark of the park. I'll never find him.

With a snarl, I wrench the compass with all my might. My jeans tear with a satisfying sound, and I race forward again. *Where is he?* I reach the end of the tents, searching wildly. A scrape of sound makes me spin. *There!* I rush forward, barely able to see his outline.

"Beat it, kid!" he says, pulling his hat lower.

"Look!" I hold up the compass, and it glints in the faint starlight. Something else glimmers too. I see the look of recognition in his eyes.

"Here..." I hold it out to him, biting back a grin when he takes it.

"Haven't seen this in years," he murmurs. Then, with both hands, he twists the top one way and the bottom the other; the compass whirrs and clicks softly as three separate layers unlock and fan out.

My mouth falls open in awe as the many glass faces catch in the starlight.

"Where did you get this, boy?" he asks.

"M….my attic! Dad said it belonged to you." Leaning closer and lowering my voice, I added, "Plus, I found a notebook with *Twice Buried, Once Found* written in it."

"Ha! Thought that stuff was long lost. When I was… When I was at war…" He says the words slowly. "My mom's house burned down, and I figured all this had gone with it."

"No, sir!" I can't help staring at him, longing to ask him about the treasure, but I'm afraid he'll disappear into the night if I do.

"Let me have a look at you." He takes my shoulders and studies my face. "You look like a modern rendition of my school photos. Greg's son? What are the chances?"

"Pretty slim, I guess. I followed you because I was sure you were my dad. But you won't doubt me a bit when you see him!" I pause with my heart in my throat. "You will see him, won't you?"

Elliot sighs deeply. "Not in public." He jerks one wide thumb toward the tents. Then he searches the dark landscape ahead. "See those two peaks right there?"

I nod rapidly.

"Walk that way, and I'll build a fire out yonder. You won't miss it. Meet me there in 20 minutes with Greg, boy."

"Oh…okay!" I say, eyeing the irresistible and very not-broken compass that's still in his hand. I stifle a groan at losing it. But it is his. "Twenty minutes."

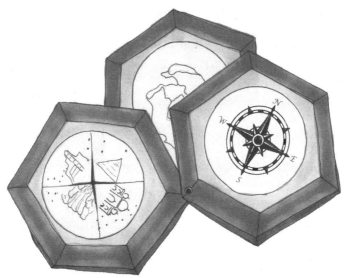

I run for the rows of tents. If the emotions I had earlier were hard to handle, adding these is like lighting a rocket! I nearly skid past our tent before bursting inside.

"Wake up!" I fairly shout, then clamp a hand over my mouth. No one can know Uncle Elliot is here but us.

My family groans at the intrusion. I rush forward and shake Dad, whispering so fast the words get all jumbled up.

"You just had a dream, Buddy. Go back to sleep."

"No!" I punch my leg, but I've got to keep quiet. "Dad, Uncle Elliot is waiting for us. We've got to go!"

By the time I convince them to get up, I'm sure we're too late; but I still turn back to grab the old notebook as we head out the door.

"How could you possibly meet…" Ethan has no volume filter when he is still waking up.

"Be quiet! Just trust me. Now hurry!" The cold night air wakes them up better than I had done.

"This is crazy," Sadie groans, rubbing her eyes.

"Here we are in the middle of the night...out following a dream," Ethan whines.

I roll my eyes, nearly prancing with excitement.

"He'll have a fire going up here a ways. You'll see." I cringe at the end of the line of tents, searching desperately for the two peaks Uncle Elliot had pointed out. *Oh, no! What if I can't find them?* I cut to the right until I'm positive that this was where we had stood talking.

"There!" I say, and relief floods through me as I make out the monstrous shoulders of the mountains.

I sure wish I'd brought a flashlight. Tripping in the dark, Mom groans behind me. "Isaiah, honey, is this some sort of wild goose chase?"

"Please, Mom, just a little farther! You'll see." But soon, doubt is pressing heavy on me too. Surely, we should have met him by now. *What if he only wanted to get rid of me? And he even took the compass too!*

"There's something!" Sadie whispers, saving me from turning back.

"Yes! See, I told you!" We draw closer to a small campfire ringed with stones. By the time we're within its circle of warmth, I've still failed to locate Elliot.

"Heard about random fire. Saw random fire. Can we go back now?" Ethan says, staring sleepily into the flames.

A branch snaps to our left, and we all flinch. Dad turns toward the sound, his features clear in the orange light.

"Greg, boy?"

Dad laughs, turning toward the voice. "I haven't heard that name in ages!"

I can barely make out Uncle Elliot's figure beyond the firelight. He'd been hiding until he was sure I had brought his nephew—my dad.

"Let me look upon you." Elliot steps from his hiding place, staring at Dad in amazement. Finally, he takes off his glasses and hat. Mom sucks in a breath; the two men look like identical twins separated by 30 years!

Dad breaks the tension by striding up and embracing Uncle Elliot. Tears shimmer in both their eyes.

Dad eventually holds Elliot at arm's length, studying him. "Remember how you used to throw me into the lake? I'd beg you to do it until you couldn't throw me one more time."

Uncle Elliot laughs in amazement.

"It's quite a treasure hunt you've led us all on. I sure wish we'd been the ones to find it though."

Elliot nods. "Still might be…"

"What's that?" Dad asks, his eyes intense.

"Just checked, it's still right where I left it two years ago. The find is a hoax."

"YES!" I leap high, pumping my fist.

Elliot grins. "That's the spirit."

"So…where did you say you came from?" Ethan asks.

Elliot's smile grows. "Didn't. Nice try though.

You've got the clues same as all the others, and I can't be unfair simply because you're family, you know."

Ethan snaps his fingers in disappointment as I slowly hold out the notebook to my great-uncle. Uncle Elliot takes it carefully, rubbing his thumb over the cover.

"Here's my question," I say. "If you wrote this clue so many years ago, why did you wait so long to tell people about the treasure?"

Uncle Elliot looks up at the wide expanse of night. "Well, that's an easy question to answer. I came to Yosemite as a teenager, and I hiked here for weeks. I fell in love with the park. I was a poor boy then, but I thought if ever I were to bury a treasure, it would be here.

I wrote the poem as a map to help me remember my personal favorite place in the entire park. Then I was drafted into the military." He swallows hard at the memory. "And then I was captured by the enemy."

Yosemite Fortune

At the word *enemy*, visions of Brock fill my mind. I cringe at the thought.

"I guess I lost myself there as a prisoner. When I finally escaped, I lived in the jungle for nearly ten years. That's when it happened…"

- 18 -

"What happened?" Sadie breathes, enraptured by the tale.

"I stumbled across an ancient native—you know the type—loincloth, long hair. He was very sick, but I nursed him back to health. From that time on, he taught me a lot. He also told me about a legend he had heard as a boy.

He said his dream was to step into the next life at the Hidden Temple. I started searching for this place called the Hidden Temple. I've always been quite good at figuring out clues, and my native friend did get to the temple before he took his last breath.

Yosemite Fortune

"Then I realized I didn't want to go out the way he had—all alone except for one strange man from across the world. Getting out the treasure took me many trips over a period of years. I had to be really careful. But going through everything I did makes a man...cautious. So, I came home and married a wonderful lady, but I kept mostly to myself."

He frowns at Dad, and a tear squeezes from the corner of his eye. "But, seeing you, Greg, makes me know I should've reached out long ago."

Dad smiles. "Well, Uncle Elliot, this is a pretty good start."

"Hang on a minute here," Ethan says with both hands on his hip. "Why are we still standing here if the treasure is still hidden?"

"In case you hadn't noticed, Ethan, it's pitch dark," Sadie says flatly.

"Do you have any children?" Mom asks.

Uncle Elliot rubs his chin. "Well, now that's an interesting question, and the answer to it means... that I'm my own grandpa." He lets the silence hang heavily as we try to absorb his statement. With a chuckle, he continues, "You see, I married a lady who's a good bit older than me, and she already had a grown daughter. Well, it wasn't long before my wife's daughter and my father fell in love and got married.

"That marriage made my dad my son-in-law, but then it got *weirder* as I realized that my daughter was now my mother-in-law. Soon enough, I had a son, and that meant he was my dad's brother-in-law, which made my son, well, *my uncle.* Then, as old as he was, my father had another child, and oddly enough, that kid was both my *grandchild* and my *brother.*

"So, my wife is my mother's mother, and although she is my wife, that makes her my grandmother too. And since I'm married to my grandmother, that means…I'm my own grandpa!" Elliot chuckles, and I stare in wonder at his recitation.

"What is that?" Sadie asks, pointing to a red flare over the mountains. "Is it sunrise?"

Elliot shakes his head. "No, my dearest great-niece, *that* is the forest fire."

My heart slams inside my chest. The glow had been so sudden, and it's so large already.

"It doesn't look good," Dad says. Then he turns to Uncle Elliot. "As much as I would love to have more time with you, I would hate to have anyone discover you're here. I don't think it would be… safe. But let's stay in touch." We all hug him, and my blood pounds with the thought of one question. *Will the fire keep us from finding the treasure?*

"Goodbye, Uncle Elliot!" I call softly, wishing he'd given back the incredible compass.

"Uncle Elliot…" His quiet voice echoes back to us. "I like the sound of that."

-19-

"Only volunteer firefighters may stay within the park boundaries. Due to the high winds, the Mono Lake fire has spread faster overnight," the ranger announces.

"Is there enough manpower to protect the park?" Mom asks.

The ranger's laugh sounds hollow. "With this wind? No."

"Why does that make a difference?" Sadie asks.

"Wind feeds the fire oxygen and carries the embers far away. Those embers can start new fires on their own. That's how fires jump over our dugout boundaries."

Yosemite Fortune

"Is digging how you'll protect Yosemite?" Dad asked.

"Yes, we've got to stop the fire with bare dirt, and then we can only hope it doesn't jump our lines."

I stare at the massive horizon; everything I can see is Yosemite. And now it's all shrouded by a thick black cloud. "How could you ever dig that much?"

The ranger slaps his thigh. "The only way to do it is with a lot of hands."

"Our hands are ready," Mom says.

Hearing her response could nearly blow me over with a feather.

"Well, never thought I'd hear you say such a thing," Dad says, staring at Mom.

"This place deserves our protection. We came to enjoy it and leaving the park when it's in danger is not right."

My heart grows warm at her words. *She's the best Mom ever.*

"Yes, fire crew, here we come!" Sadie shouts.

I turn, watching the flood of people leaving the park. I know it's better if most of them go, but without them, can Yosemite possibly survive? A pickup truck pulls out, and I see a man in its bed with a megaphone.

"That's Dave!" Sadie and Ethan say together.

"People!" Dave's voice reverberates through Curry Village. Everyone turns to look at him. "I'm talking to you, treasure hunters! That's right, listen up! You came here to get something from Yosemite—to take the treasure. Now look at you! Running away when this incredible place needs you most. Every single one of you has marveled at Half Dome, El Capitan, the waterfalls! Don't let it be destroyed, brothers and sisters! Together we can save it!" Dave's free hand is in the air, beckoning the people. His face is even redder than normal.

"Save Yosemite!" Sadie shouts, caught up in the moment. Someone in the crowd echoes her, then another, until the voices unite and thunder out a battle cry against the fire that's raging this way.

"Save Yosemite!"
"Save Yosemite!"
"Save Yosemite!"

The chant only grows, and my voice is strong in the middle of it. I glance over to see tears in the ranger's eyes. These wild places belong to all of us, and we'll do our best to protect them. Dave's voice sounds in the megaphone, "Firefighters, report to the ranger station at the far end of Curry Village for instructions."

The sea of people parts, and I recognize a bunch of the treasure hunters I had watched suspiciously before. Those feelings melt away now as we all move toward the ranger station.

"Save Yosemite!"

Suddenly, the treasure of gold pales in comparison to the treasure that is Yosemite.

-20-

    My shovel bites into the rocky soil. The scraping sound seems like it's the only one I've ever heard. The shovel's sudden stop rips open one of my many blisters. I wipe sooty sweat from my forehead with my forearm, ignoring the pain.

    Smoke hangs heavy all around. The acrid scent burns my lungs and eyes. Sadie's shovel barely scrapes anything beside me. We've fought to save Yosemite for two full days. Exhaustion can't even begin to explain how I feel. We'd started at the north end of the park where the fire had raged in, and our combined forces had turned aside the Mono Lake fire. But the unpredictable wind keeps pushing the flames back toward the park. We're in the south section of the park now, working north of Silver Apron.

An empty laugh escapes my dry lips. We're only one valley away from where I'm certain the treasure lies. *If the flames reach the cache, I guess it will turn into one puddle of gold.*

Sadie rests her cheek on the shovel, her face streaked with soot, her eyes red from the burning smoke. Ethan is spread-eagled on the ground.

"I'm thirsty…." His voice sounds painful as it rasps past his throat.

The loud scratch of a shovel beside me makes me flinch. Even turning my head slowly feels like too much energy has been expended.

"Brody?" I ask, turning around to look for Brock.

"He's not here; I slipped away from them. Fighting this fire is more important than what my dad is doing. I brought some water." He pulls bottles from his pack, offering one to Sadie first.

"Thank you, Brody," she says.

Mine is gone in four seconds, and I feel like life is returning as I down the whole bottle.

Still lying on the ground, Ethan drains his bottle. "What is that sound?" he asks.

"All I hear are the flames," I choke out the words. "Maybe it's more rock exploding in the heat." At first, the sound had scared us all, but now I can ignore it.

"No, I hear a motor," he says.

Now I see what he is hearing and stare at the ancient fire truck that was once red. A huge water cannon is mounted on the top. Someone can operate the foot pedals that control when the water comes out. The oversized wheels on the old truck enable it to be driven to the front lines. I notice its motor is barely a purr.

"Yep. I hear another motor," Ethan announces. He has his ear pressed to the ground. "And… something else."

"You cannot possibly hear anything through the ground," I say. But somehow, he convinces us all to lie down with him—even Brody. Don't ask me how he does it; *he's Ethan.*

With one ear turned skyward, I hear the singing of chainsaws and then the crash of a tree as Dad and Dave cut them down to create an empty 40-feet-wide fire barrier. I never really understood how wide that distance could be before.

I plug that ear and strain to hear with the other. Ethan's right! I can almost hear the rumble of an engine. Then I do hear another sound—almost like pebbles when I throw them into the water.

Dave gives out a loud whoop, and I sit up. "The cavalry has arrived, boys!"

Dave is all streaked with black soot, and he's dripping sweat as he leans on one massive leg propped on the tree he had just felled.

I follow his gaze down the valley where a flash of bright yellow shows through the trees.

"A bulldozer!" Mom exclaims with one hand over her heart. The heavy machine rumbles up and lowers its blade. My mouth hangs open as we watch it clear a swath that would've taken us hours to make.

"Go, baby, go!" Ethan shouts. We're all revived by the bulldozer's presence. Or maybe it's the hope the machine brings along with it—as if maybe now we have a chance of holding back this fire.

A female ranger leaps off the far side of the machine. "The frontline is coming! We've got less than ten minutes until the fire sweeps full force past us! Fight, people. Fight hard!"

I look up to see the sky is as black as midnight. The hissing crackle of a pine tree catching fire grows until the entire tree explodes into flames. I look back over my shoulder at the 40 feet of mostly bare dirt. *This beast will not be stopped!* The smoke rolls thicker and thicker as more trees explode so close that I leap back, ash raining down all around us.

That strange sound comes again like pebbles, hundreds of them. Then a shrill cry rips through the air, and that's when I see the first one galloping toward us.

"Mustangs!" Sadie cries as the soot-streaked herd runs hard before the flames. Sweat drips from their chests, and foam has formed around their exhausted mouths. A massive white stallion with red patches leaps the tree Dave had dropped, then more follow, flowing like water! *The herd must be at least 200 horses strong!*

Shocked, the ranger's hands are on her cheeks. "That's the Mono Lake herd 26 miles from home!"

More trees explode, and the intense roar of the flames drowns out their desperate hoofbeats.

"Run!" Sadie screams wildly at the horses. *Only a few feet remain between them and the flames!* I droop as the last mustang finally gallops past the safety zone.

"Oh, no, no, no, NO!" Sadie is staring hard into the fire, her face white. One more brown-and-white paint mustang bursts through the thickest smoke. Exhausted and trembling, the horse stumbles, and nearly goes down. I stop breathing as she struggles in the deadly heat.

"Come on!" I shout, urging her forward.

Straight ahead, flames already lick up a tree trunk. I can see the mare is too far into the fire... *She'll never make it past that burning tree!* Her eyes roll white with fear as she surges over a boulder. Her hooves miss the landing, and her nose scrapes the ground as she struggles for balance. The tree between us hisses, crackling with angry energy. Its branches explode with that familiar sound of the entire top of the tree snapping off.

Sadie's scream seems to contain all of our terror as we watch the mare stumble below the falling tree. The horse's head comes up at Sadie's piercing cry, and the sound seems to give her another burst of speed.

Time slows down as her hooves ping on the rocky ground, and the pine needles find all the oxygen they need to burn as the treetop plummets toward the mustang. Like a racer at the finish line, her muscles bunch, and she leaps the now burning log that Dave had cut. The treetop crashes down next to her, and a scorching branch snags in her white tail.

"NO!" Sadie screams even louder as the mare's tail kindles. Tears stream down Sadie's face as she turns, racing for the old fire truck. She hits the ladder at full speed, scrambling up, grasping the huge turret handles, wailing as she tries to turn the water cannon toward the mustang.

She's too small! Just for fun, I had tried earlier to turn the water cannon, and I hadn't been able to budge it one inch.

Sadie sags, knowing the mare is lost if she fails.

Suddenly, a form emerges from the black rolling smoke, and I see Dave running like a streak of lightning. His mouth opens in a shout that I can't hear over the roar of the fire. His face is beet red and black with ash.

The truck rocks wildly as he climbs the ladder, gripping the handles with Sadie, and together they strain to turn the turret. With a sharp metallic screech, it swings free.

"Now!" Dave thunders, and Sadie stomps the water pedal.

A long spear of water traces behind the mare's flaming tail.

"GO!" I scream, watching the flames grow.

Dave wrenches the handles harder. The mustang sweeps between me and the truck. She's so close I can hear her shuddering breath and the sizzle of her tail, the flames creeping upward. She turns her head my way as she runs, catching sight of the fire. Her eyes roll white again. We're all screaming and willing the water forward.

Suddenly, the water cannon swings closer, shooting up over the mare's heaving sides. She runs through this stream, extinguishing the flames! As quickly as she came, she's gone. Nothing is now between me and the water cannon, which knocks me flat on my back. I shiver in its icy blast.

Dave throws back his head with a primal victory cry as I scramble away from the water.

"YES!" Sadie shouts. The trail of her tears is

plain on her sooty cheeks. She turns, gripping Dave in one of her surprisingly strong bear hugs. Then she leaps up for a high five.

"Let's fight some more fire, little lady!" Dave shouts, straining to turn the cannon back toward the fire line. Mom and Dad rush over and begin checking me for injuries.

"I'm fine, Mom, and so is this part of Yosemite."

Mom tries to sniff back a tear and fails. More flow down her cheeks, and I can't hold back my own. *We've done it! No matter what happens later, we had stood our ground and won!*

-21-

Sadie is hugging me tight, and I wrap my arms around her. "Good job, sis! You saved her."

She laughs, grinning at me. "Thanks, but it was mostly Dave."

"Not so! You were his inspiration." I lower my voice. "I didn't think a guy that big could move that fast!"

"That's true!" She giggles.

"I hear something," Ethan says. Once again, he's lying spread-eagled on the ground.

"Oh, no," I say.

Brody tries to cover a smile as if he's not sure he's allowed to do such a thing.

"No, I hear it too."

We turn, searching the charred battle line.

"Something is moving," Brody adds.

"There!" Sadie rushes forward. Leave it to my little sister to be the first to spot any creature.

"Turtles!" she cries. Stooping down, Brody quickly joins her.

"Watch out! They can bite," he cautions protectively.

"Oh, come on," she croons, "I know how to hold turtles." She's already got one in each hand. "I wonder if they are box turtles?" She's using that famous tone that soothes even the wildest beast.

The ranger gasps with delight when she comes over. "No, these are actually Western pond turtles, the only surviving species of turtle still living in Yosemite. They're usually most common in the Hetch Hetchy area."

"Hetch Hetchy?" Ethan lifts his head. "What kind of name is that?"

The ranger shrugs. "I guess if you think that

name is weird, you haven't yet visited Poopenaut Valley."

"Poopenaut?" His laugh is infectious, and soon even Brody is chuckling.

"Here, you hold this one." Sadie hands one turtle to Brody as she picks up the third.

"I think we had better get these little fellas to some water. After all, they just survived a wildfire, and they happen to be a rare species," the ranger declares.

"Oh, no! This one is burned."

We pack our things as Sadie and the ranger check on the turtles. Soon, we load up into the back of the old fire truck, and Sadie sets a pond turtle in my hands. His little beak makes him look as if he's smiling. "I shall name you Happy."

"And the name of mine is Fearless," Sadie adds. "How about yours, Brody?"

He's quiet, studying the turtle, and then he quietly says, "I think his name is Freedom."

Sadie, Ethan, and I look at each other. Brody

had risked so much to come here and help us. I'm sure freedom is what Brody longs for the most. We hike down in the valley until the ranger calls for a halt.

"Come on, kids, let's get these turtles home." We follow her into the woods.

"You want to have a race?" she asks and then stops a good distance from a small pond.

"I, for one, am Poopenaut!" Ethan throws back his head with laughter.

"I didn't mean *you* would race; I meant the turtles would race. Come on you three, line up. Now hold them high enough that they see the water."

The moment Happy sees the glistening surface, he starts paddling like crazy. "Ouch!" I say. *His claws are super sharp!*

"On the count of three. Let them go! One, two, three!" the ranger instructs.

Happy takes off into the grass. Ethan is on his hands and knees, narrating.

"And Fearless pulls ahead, but the race is far from over, people! Happy is creeping up on the left side, and he might take the lead from Fearless. Oh! Now both of them have stopped for a snack. Hold on, people! It's Freedom pulling closer. Freedom is now in the lead! FREEDOM! It's Freedom for the win!"

We hear a splash as the little turtle disappears below the water.

Happy and Fearless hear the sound of Freedom's splash, and soon knowing that turtles had ever been here at all is impossible. Who knew a race at a snail's pace could be so much fun?

-22-

We sleep like rocks at the temporary camp the rangers have set up on the far side of the Mist Trail footbridge.

I groan when something shakes me.

I swat at it. "No, five more minutes…"

"You don't have five minutes." The sound of Brody's urgent voice snaps me wide awake. He had gone back to his dad and brother late last night where they're still camped in the tight valley between Mount Broderick and Liberty—where the treasure lies nearby.

"Did they find it?" I whisper.

He shakes his head. "No, this is bigger news."

One side of my nose wrinkles up. "What could be more important than that?"

"We found an injured mustang foal at the far end of the valley." I lean in to catch his lowered tone. "He's hurt bad." His eyes drop to the rocky ground. "Dad says he'll die…natural selection, you know." Brodie's eyes find mine again, and they are burning with passion. "But I say the foal needs help."

I nod, my thoughts running wild. Suddenly, my head snaps up. "The wind has stopped!"

Brody smiles. "Yes, that means the fire has weakened, and it's moving east—away from here."

I study Sadie in her sleeping bag near Mom and Dad. I bite my lip. *What would it do to her if the foal doesn't make it?*

"Anyway, he'll die if someone doesn't help him."

"Who will die?" Sadie asks, sitting up.

I sigh, knowing that keeping her away from the injured animal will be impossible. Brody's cheeks grow red as he looks at her.

"A mustang foal."

She gasps, already 100 percent dedicated to the task. "Let's go!"

"Ummm…we have a slight problem." Brody swallows hard.

"Problem?" Ethan says, wiping sleep from his eyes.

"He's at the end of the *valley*."

We all look at each other.

"So, your dad won't let us in," Ethan says.

Brody nods. "But I think he'll be busy fu…" He chokes back the word, a sheen of fear appearing in his eyes. "I think he'll be busy elsewhere."

"So, Brock is the problem." Sadie shivers as she says his name.

"Actually, I worked out a deal with Brock. He'll let the three of you into the valley on one condition—an impossible one." As we lean closer, he tilts his head toward Sadie. "Your sister has to beat him in a foot race."

"Me?" Sadie squeaks. "Why not Ethan?"

Brody shrugs. "Trust me, no one can reason

with my brother. One thing is for sure; he doesn't like to lose."

Sadie clenches her jaw. "I'll do it," she declares.

"Oh, no. I don't trust him—not one bit," I say sternly.

"I'll be all right," Sadie insists. "I'll beat him, you'll see."

Brodie's eyebrows lift. "He is really fast."

"We don't have any time to waste. I'll ask Mom and Dad if we can go on a hike for a while." She moves off before I can resist the idea any longer. I glare at the sun, flaring red through the hanging haze of smoke.

Sadie follows Mom over to the coffee station where the rangers have already gathered. I know the second Sadie turns toward us that Mom has said yes.

"The fire risk is almost at zero. Mom says we can go if we stay in the valley and come right back here."

A knot forms in my stomach. "Are you sure Brock won't hurt her?" I question.

Yosemite Fortune

"If it was one of you two boys, I wouldn't have any guarantee. But he won't hurt a girl; he only wants a chance to beat you all."

"Well, he won't," Sadie says.

Brody can't cover the admiration in his gaze. "Let's go then."

-23-

Sadie is stretching her legs as I study the course that Brock has laid out. He's planned everything to his advantage. At one section, they will run up a series of boulders that will be simple for his long legs and far harder for Sadie's. At the turnaround, there's a tall rock that they'll have to go over.

"I don't know about this," I mutter, my chest feeling tight.

Brody comes over and leans close, whispering to Sadie; then he heads back over to his brother. Sadie turns to us with one hand clamped over her mouth.

"What did he say?" Ethan is as suspicious as I am.

"He said not to be afraid of Brock. They share the middle name of Lee."

"Brody Lee," I say flatly, not understanding why she is stifling a giggle.

"Yes, and that means it's Brock Lee."

"Broccoli?" Ethan says.

"Yes! I can't possibly be afraid of a boy whose name is Brock Lee Smith."

"Maybe that's why he's so mean," Ethan says, snapping his fingers.

"Anyway..." Sadie says, holding out her hand to Ethan, "give me a taffy."

He pats all his pockets. "Um, I can't."

"Come on, hand it over," she insists.

"No, seriously, I don't have any!"

Her face goes pale. "Bu...bu...but that was my plan. I have to have sugar in order to beat him!" Her voice gets higher-pitched with every word.

Ethan's mouth hangs open, horrified. I stick my hand in my pocket, fingering what used to be the watermelon taffy I had snatched away from Sadie a few days ago. With all the digging and shoveling, it had inched out of the wrapper and is now smashed into my pocket fuzz. The water cannon had sort of turned everything into cement.

Sadie is starting to lose it. Her hands are flapping wildly, and she can barely form the words she wants to say. "He… We… I can't let that foal die!" She swallows hard.

It's bad if I do…and worse if I don't. I scrape what used to be the taffy off the bottom of my pocket. When I hold it out, Sadie stares at it with one side of her nose wrinkled up. "What is that?"

"It was taffy…in another life."

She sucks in a breath and kisses my cheek. "You are the best brother!"

She takes it and starts picking the fuzz out of it. "Oh, this is gross." She nods and says to herself, "It's for a good cause, Sadie. Think of the foal. Think of the foal."

"Listen, only eat half of it, okay?"

She glares at me. "…and risk failure?"

"No! I'm thinking the more you eat, the less chance we have of victory," Ethan states.

"Precisely, the more sugar you eat, the crazier you'll be," I add.

"Listen," she says, pointing at us with the fuzzy taffy. "I know I have a track record of being a little wild on sugar."

We glare at her for the gross understatement.

"Okay, a *lot* wild. But listen, I've never had a dying horse on the other end. *You know me.* You know how important saving that baby mustang is to me." Then before we can argue any more, she stuffs the taffy into her mouth and swallows without chewing.

"Oh, gross!" Her stomach heaves, and I think we might see the taffy again.

"I can't believe I ate that!"

But Ethan and I look at each other. Horrified, I whirl toward Brock and Brody. "Race! NOW!" I demand as Ethan starts a countdown from 10…9…8…

"What's the hurry?" Brock asks.

"Seven, six…" Ethan says. He watches Sadie as a shiver runs down her spine.

"It's now, or the deal is off!" I shout at Brock.

Sadie toes up to the starting line, bouncing from foot to foot.

"Four…three…"

"You'd better get ready!" My shout makes Brock step next to Sadie.

"Two…one!" Ethan yells, "Go! Go, Sadie, go!"

Brock takes off like a jackrabbit, but Sadie twirls in a little circle. Her eyes catch mine, and I know the sugar is in control. With the wild whoop, she sets off for the boulder staircase. Brock is already halfway up, and he's struggling with the longer leaps.

Sadie's pace changes at the bottom. Instead of jumping onto the first rock, she sets both hands on it, then goes on all fours running like an ape.

"Go Sadie-monkey!" Ethan cheers.

"She's faster than I figured," Brody notes.

"You have no idea!" I exclaim.

Sadie has nearly caught up with Brock at the top, but he doesn't know she's right on his heels.

"Whaaahooo!" she yells, plunging down the hill, her legs a blur.

"Hey!" Brock shouts when Sadie passes him, anger clearly written on his face.

Ahead, Sadie leaps for the boulder near the turn. She looks sort of like a splat ball as she sticks to its side for a moment and then sort of slides down.

Brock whoops as he ramps off a smaller boulder to one side, then up onto the big one. He had planned how he would make those leaps.

But Sadie is already regrouping, rubbing her hands together with a crazy gleam in her eyes.

"Careful, Sadie, careful!" I can't hold back the words.

She launches toward the boulder, bends forward into a handspring, then she soars straight up, her arms spread wide, soaring over it like an eagle. I gasp, and Brody exclaims, "Wooowww!" I nearly collapse as she rolls into a landing on our side of the rock. She comes up on one knee, her eyes locking savagely on Brock as he races toward us.

Sadie grins.

"Stay on course!" I bellow, hoping that the sugar won't make her deviate. "Stay on course!"

It's as if she's been shot from a rocket while Brock is standing still instead of running like the wind. She lets out another yell, starting to swerve.

"STAY ON COURSE!" I thunder. She straightens her course and passes Brock so fast his shirt flaps as she goes by. She flashes past me, sidestepping my desperate grab. "NO!"

Ethan is like a human spider web as he jumps in front of her, his arms and legs spread wide.

They go down hard, but Ethan breaks her fall nicely. I leap on top, and we wrestle with her until she finally goes still.

"Did I win?" I hear her real voice again; "Sugar Sadie" is gone. Ethan and I let her up.

"You did it!" Brody exclaims in awe.

Brock is heaving in breaths and declares hotly, "No, she didn't. She cheated! Nobody's faster than me. You can't pass!"

Sadie's eyes narrow as she glares at Brock. Somehow, she reminds me of a porcupine even though she has no quills.

"What..." she hisses the word, "did you say?"

"You can't pass!" Brock insists, puffing out his chest.

Her eyes are mere slits, and Ethan and I back away. Her stance gives Brock a bit of a pause.

Sadie stalks toward him, her breath coming faster. "Don't... You... Dare..." She's reached him now, but she doesn't stop walking, her pointer finger smashing into his chest with every word, "ever say that again!" she growls. Brock backs up as if she's punching him. Even though she's so much shorter than he is, Brock steps to the side, his eyes wide.

Maybe my sister does have one quill, and that one was just enough!

-24-

Sadie strides down into the valley, her hands going wild as she talks to herself. I can't catch her rapid-fire words, and I'm fairly sure Brock Lee is glad he can't either. Ethan and I break after her.

"The nerve of some people!" she fumes. We hike in silence for a long time, letting her cool off.

"I sure wish we had started counting steps at the mouth of the valley," Ethan suddenly comments.

"Why?" Sadie asks.

"Um…1001 steps, though tiring, are not fatal. 1001 steps!"

"Oh, boys! We are NOT here for treasure! We have a foal to save."

I look at Ethan, knowing I've been thinking the same way. He and I are scanning like crazy as we walk. *Maybe one of us will catch sight of the treasure box!*

Sadie suddenly gasps. "There it is!"

"Where?" Ethan and I snap to attention, desperately looking for a small box.

"Right there! How can you miss him?"

"Oh, right," I say, catching sight of the mustang foal. His coat is white and red-patched, like the stallion leading the herd. Well, I guess he used to be white; now he's ashy gray.

"He's Firefly's baby," Sadie says softly.

"Who is Firefly?"

"The mare whose tail was on fire, of course! He looks exactly like her," Sadie gasps. "I bet that's why she was so far behind the herd! She was looking for her foal. I'm going to need your survival bracelets."

Sadie starts unwinding hers. Our bracelets, which are made of parachute cord (paracord), contain over 20 feet of woven nylon cord after they're undone. The paracord has many uses. I unclip mine and start to unwind it as we quietly approach the barely standing foal. His perfect little nose has drooped heavily toward the ground, and he's swaying as if the wind will knock him over. He doesn't even try to run as we approach. I grimace when I spot a deep cut over one of his shoulders.

"You poor baby," Sadie croons. Then she starts to sing, and the little foal's ears twitch at the sweet sound. Ever so slowly, Sadie eases the rope over his neck. His skin begins to twitch, but his eyes don't open.

"Sadie," I say guardedly. "He's in worse shape than I thought. Please don't fall in love with him, okay?"

"Too late," she whispers. Her eyes are limitless pools of tears. "We must get him back. He needs a veterinarian."

"What do we do?" Ethan asks. I can tell even he is moved by the little guy's condition.

"You two push him from behind, and I'll use

the rope to tug from the front. Oh, he's so hot! He must have a fever. Come on, boys. Time is ticking."

What on earth have we gotten into now? Sadie has always been attached to animals, but this care for the foal is something completely different—even deeper. I can see it in her eyes.

"Come on, Ember," she coaxes. "We'll get you all better."

I bite my lip. *If Ember doesn't survive, what will that loss do to Sadie?*

-25-

Sweat rolls off my eyebrows. Ember isn't really standing on his own anymore. It's Ethan and me holding him up. For being so little, he sure is heavy.

A tear slips from Sadie's eyes as she struggles to help the foal balance. The only way forward is over a fallen log near the valley entrance. Sadie picks up one front hoof and lifts it over.

"Hold him up!" she cries as the foal lurches to one side.

"We're…" I grit out.

"Trying!" Ethan finishes in an equally desperate tone. Ember nearly falls down, but Sadie rushes to get his other front leg over the log. His little hoof slams down on the far side of the log with a metallic clink.

We all freeze, bent in awkward positions, trying to keep the foal from collapsing. Wide-eyed, we stare at each other. *Only one thing in this valley could possibly make that sound—treasure.*

"Don't show any reaction." I whisper, barely moving my lips. We are right next to the racetrack, so I know Brock and possibly his father are watching us struggle. My skin crawls at the thought. *Do we grab it and try to fight our way out? That might not end well.*

"Well, what's it look like?" Ethan barely breathes the words. Sadie only moves her eyes, still bent low, holding up Ember.

"Small metal box. Brown, covered in moss, tucked right under the log," she whispers. Ember groans and starts to fall. He's nearly limp but somehow we get him completely over the log.

"Don't look, don't look, don't look!" Ethan is repeating under his breath as we pass by.

All my willpower is required to obey his chant. Every fiber of my being wants to see what is in that small box.

Somehow, we make it out of the valley, and Ember promptly collapses on Ethan.

"Ugh!" He squeaks. "I'm being squished by a giant limp noodle!"

"At least it's not a giant hot dog."

My muscles burn as I roll Ember just enough for Ethan to wiggle free. Sadie is already holding Ember's head in her lap. Her tears are running like Vernal Falls, dripping onto his head.

"Hurry! Run for Mom!" she cries. Ethan takes off, making me wonder if he could have beaten Brock…Lee.

Soon, Ethan returns, running in front of a group of people scattered behind him in a V-formation. Mom is sprinting, nearly surpassing Dad.

"Mama! He needs help!" Sadie wails.

I wring my hands as Ember groans. *This is what I was afraid of! It will break Sadie inside if he…*

"Come on, Ember!" I whisper, placing both hands on his hot fur.

Someone pushes through the crowd. "I'm a vet! Let me through!"

The woman is streaked with ash like the rest of us. A long reddish braid is slung over one shoulder. Checking Ember's mouth, she mutters, "He can't be more than a month and half old.... He needs an IV right away."

She pulls off her pack and sets to work. Ethan and I pull Dad to one side.

"We found it," I whisper softly.

"It's right there!" Ethan adds, too loud for my liking.

"Shhh! The clue must have meant 1001 feet... not steps. It's barely inside the valley."

"Greg, we need you!" Mom calls.

Dad leans close. "Sounds like this is something *men* need to care for after dark. My eyes go wide at his meaning. "We go for the treasure tonight."

-26-

Turns out there's an old horse stable in Yosemite Valley that's been closed for a few years; but as I look into the stall, I'm glad Sadie and Ember have a safe place to rest. Sadie's head lies on his neck as they sleep.

"If he pulls through tonight, there may be hope for saving him," the vet says softly to Mom.

"*If...*" Mom says. She has a pained look on her face as she watches Sadie. Dad steps into the barn. He only says one word. But it's all we need to hear.

"Men."

A shiver ripples up my nerves. I think of Uncle Elliot's escaping prison, hiding in the jungle. Now his family is breaking into a sort of prison only to escape with his treasure. I don't feel my feet even touch the ground as we follow Dad into the sunset evening.

Soon, we are shadows in the night. The face paint we'd applied still feels heavy on my cheeks as we pass Vernal Falls in silence. The moonlight provides just enough light to walk by. Dad stops next to Silver Apron.

"Here's the plan." His low voice sends a shiver down my spine.

Ethan stuffs a banana taffy in his mouth.

"I thought you were out of those."

"I restocked. Keep 'em in my sleeping bag."

I roll my eyes.

"Seriously, boys. We've got to go silently and quickly from here on out. I have no doubt that Mr. Smith will go to any length to keep us out of the valley and try to get the treasure from us once we have it."

I swallow hard at the thought.

"Ethan, you will be the lookout."

"Why?" he says, clearly distressed at his post.

"Oh, come on, this entire foray into the valley hinges on the lookout. Without a sentry, we wouldn't have a chance."

Ethan sighs.

"Well, it's the lookout, and this should do the trick." Dad pulls a small metal box from his pack.

"Mom's bacon box?" I ask my upper lip pulled back in a question.

"You brought bacon? Uncle Greg, you are the best!" Ethan slings an arm around Dad's shoulders.

"It's empty," Dad says.

"Nooo!" Ethan sinks to his knees.

"What's it for, anyway?" I don't see what good Mom's bear-proof meat storage container is going to do us.

"Well, with a few..." Dad bends low, scooping up a handful of mud. "Additions..." He smears the box with a thick layer of muck.

"Aunt Ruth is going to get you for that," Ethan

says. "You of all people knows she allows no one to touch her bacon box."

Dad simply flashes a wild grin. "And some more extra weight..." He loads the container with pebbles and rocks. "It should make a pretty good double for our treasure box if our sortie goes south."

"South?" Ethan asks. "Um...I thought the valley is to the east."

"No, I mean, if our plan goes awry," Dad answers, shaking his head at Ethan.

"Ooohhhh..." Ethan adds, nodding his head.

But I can see he still doesn't get it.

Then he rubs his belly. "Bacon and hash browns." One eyelid slides shut. "Yum!"

"Okay, here's the plan." Dad stuffs the dirty box back into his pack. "Ethan enters the valley first."

"YES!" He pumps his fist in the air.

"Silently and carefully," Dad adds.

"Aw."

"You climb the tallest tree with a view of the treasure."

"I know just the one," he declares.

"Great! Isaiah and I will give you ten minutes to get into position. Then, we come for the treasure. Ethan, if you see anything, hoot like an owl."

"Sure. Whooo, whooo. Yep, I got this."

"If they see us, we use the bacon box as a decoy." Dad whispers a few more words, and a shot of adrenaline courses down my arms.

-27-

I'm on my stomach only two yards from the treasure. I look over at Dad and point without a sound. His mouth opens when he catches sight of only the corner showing past the thick grass under the log.

We army crawl forward, all the while listening for the hoot of an owl. Together, we reach out and touch the box. Dad's grin shows his teeth, a brilliant white against the black face paint. With utmost silence, he opens his pack and withdraws the bacon box.

Reverently, I lift the treasure—at least I try to lift the box. Its weight has sunk the treasure deep into the mud over time, and the grass is tangled, making it difficult.

I flinch at a breath of sound. Dad and I freeze, our ears straining. The soft, airy sound comes again. It must be a bird's wings flapping in the night. Grimacing, I set the box in Dad's pack. Dirt crumbles everywhere. I close the zipper with trembling fingers. The whisper of sound echoes again, and I begin to wonder if an owl really is flying around, and if so, how could we tell his hoot from Ethan's voice anyway?

Dad carefully tucks the bacon box under his arm as if it is the treasure.

"Stealing something that's not yours?" Mr. Smith's low growl makes all the blood drain from my face.

He's right there—on the other side of the log.

Dad and I stare at him in horror.

"*Whooo! Whoooo!*" Ethan nearly screams.

Dad lets out a sharp breath, then takes off running to the right. I twist, crouching low as Mr.

Smith leaps for Dad. With a bellow, they go down in a tangle.

"Isaiah!" Dad cries.

In the scant moonlight, I see the bacon box soaring into the air.

I pounce for it, uttering a husky cry as it hits me in the chest. I can barely breathe now. Brock suddenly emerges from the trees and comes toward me with his flashing speed. I take off, but I know I'll never outrun him. I'm built for strength—definitely not speed. Desperate, I search for some way out, but he's *right there*, his breath coming down my neck.

Locking up my legs, I skid to a halt, then bend low. Brock can't stop in time, so he flips over me into the dirt with a grunt. Grinning, I take off back toward the valley entrance. But three steps later, Brock flattens me with a flying tackle from the side.

No. Air. I fruitlessly fight for breath, painfully aware as Brock holds me down, and Mr. Smith wrenches the box from my grip.

Dad is hot on his heels, and he snags one of Mr. Smith's legs. The big man goes down hard. *He might have that limp for real now.*

The box skids across a rocky patch. A wild rebel yell echoes. I finally catch my breath as Ethan's string-bean frame catapults toward the box. Still, I can't shout to tell him that Brock is doing the same thing.

They leap at the same time, but Ethan's on the bottom! I scramble up, rushing forward to grasp Brock's legs. Holding Brock as he tries to throw me off takes everything I have. Somehow, Ethan manages to weasel out from under us with the box tucked under his arm like a football.

Brock wiggles free from my hold and gains on Ethan. He leaps, Ethan's legs tangle up, and they both go down hard.

That looked like it hurt.

"Men!" Dad thunders. Ethan rolls so Brock can snatch the box. We scatter, rushing for the narrow mouth of "the cradle."

A figure steps out in front of us, and we skid to a halt. *It's Brody.* Having no idea what he will do, my heart is pounding. A slow smile curls one side of his mouth. He steps to the side and waves us through the gap. I nod at him as we pass.

"Tell Sadie I said goodbye."

-28-

"I can't wait to get to our tent and look at the treasure!" Ethan is nearly dancing with glee.

"Oh, that's the last place we're going to put this box." Dad puffs as we rush across the footbridge.

"AARRRGGH!"

My eyes go wide as an angry shout ripples over us from the canyon.

"I guess Smith opened it," I whisper. We look at each other and pick up the pace, running past Silver Apron and then Vernal Falls.

He'll be hunting us now, and Dad's right: we dare not leave the treasure in our tent. Suddenly, the entire world feels like an enemy. *We can't trust any-*

one! When we finally reach Yosemite Valley, Dad directs us toward the stables.

I swallow hard, my stomach queasy as we enter. *What if Ember didn't make it?* A large group of people have gathered in front of his stall. Mom is standing among them. She wipes a tear, and I rush forward, pressing my face against the metal bars.

Sadie is holding Ember's beautiful head as he groans deeply with every breath. Tears are coursing down her cheeks. I slide the door open and hurry forward, wrapping my arms around Sadie from behind. Everything else is forgotten in this life-and-death struggle before me.

"He's going to make it," I whisper into her hair. I want to tell Sadie about the treasure, but the vet steps in, replacing Ember's IV bag.

"Come on, little guy, fight hard," she whispers.

A few more people step into the stall, still conversing. "The Mono Lake herd of mustangs are resting near Glacier Point, but they can't stay in Yosemite."

The ranger rubs her forehead. "We can push them back toward Mono Lake with helicopters, but I'm afraid doing so will be a death sentence for them."

"How so?" Mom asks.

"Their entire habitat just burned, and it will be months until the land can support them again."

"Can't someone feed them hay until then?"

"Enough hay to feed over 200 horses, plus the manpower to do it, would cost a fortune."

I look sharply at Dad near the far end of the stall.

"NO!" Sadie cries. "They can't all die! The fire wasn't their fault!" She's trembling as I continue to hold her. She tucks Ember's head closer, sobbing. She's exhausted from fighting the fire, and now the weight of the Mono Lake herd's future is dragging her even lower. Mom places a hand on Ember's thin neck, holding back tears.

"Then there's this little guy…if he lives. What will we do with him?" the ranger asks.

"Could…" Mom hesitates. "Could we adopt him?" Sadie's head snaps up.

"The Bureau of Land Management has jurisdiction over him, but yes, I'm sure you could adopt him for a fee."

Sadie gasps, and Mom laughs nervously. "I don't think we can separate the girl and the horse."

-29-

I blink, breathing in a strange smell. *Horse scent.*

I roll on the soft wood chips. Ember isn't groaning! *Oh no!* I crawl over to where Sadie is fast asleep next to him, holding my breath. I feel his ribs. *He's alive.* I slump in relief. And he's not hot like he had been last night, and his breathing is slow and steady.

Sadie's eyes slide open. "Was I dreaming? Did Mom really say we can adopt him?"

"Ha! She did!" I bite my lip, knowing Sadie's entire world is right here in this stall. The door rolls open, and the vet and Mom step into the stall. Sadie rushes into Mom's arms.

"My own horse!"

"Dad said yes too, but Ember has got to pull through first."

The vet gasps. "His fever has broken!"

Happy tears are now flowing down Sadie's face.

"Can you stay with him for a little while?" Mom asks the vet.

"Of course."

We follow Mom outside, and the treasure hunt comes back with a rush! Dad motions us toward a small stall that's half filled with sawdust. Ethan steps out, nodding, excitement burning.

"Sadie," Dad whispers. "We got it."

"Got what?"

Dad steps forward, digging deep in the wood pulp as Ethan slides the door shut behind us. We all gather around the small box, weathered and old. Dad forces the latch open with a squeak. He eases up the lid, and we all gasp as the dim light reveals a shimmering load of golden coins and red stones that must be rubies. I see one huge diamond!

"We're rich!" Ethan breathes.

-30-

"This is what I was afraid of…" the vet groans.

We've gotten Ember on his feet; but no matter how hard we try, he will not take milk from a bottle.

"Why won't he eat?" Sadie cries as we struggle to keep Ember standing.

"Well, he's stubborn and wild, which is a huge part of why he made it through the night. But that's also why he won't drink from anything but his mother." The vet sets the huge bottle on the floor with a sigh.

"I will have to force-feed him. The process is quite unpleasant, so I think you'd all better leave until I finish."

Sadie shakes her head. "I'm not leaving him."

"Okay, but you must understand that if he doesn't eat, he'll die. And if I get the feeding tube into his lungs instead of his stomach…he will die. We will run that risk with every feeding."

Sadie bites her lip hard, and my stomach does a flip. By the time Miss Sue forces the long tube down one of Ember's nostrils and down, down, down into his stomach, I'm feeling a little green.

"It's okay; it's okay," Sadie murmurs, grimacing as she pets the foal.

We all sigh in relief as Sue pulls out the tube. Ember shakes his head, but he takes a step forward! We all cheer for him, and then Sadie asks cautiously. "How long does he need to drink milk?"

Miss Sue answers, "At least for three more months—four times a day."

We're all quiet, thinking of repeating the force-feeding 372 more times.

Miss Sue shrugs. "The best thing for Ember is his mama."

-31-

Ethan rushes into the barn the next morning after we've force-fed Ember three more times. He's out of breath. "Two things!" he pants, "one…our tent has been completely ransacked!"

"Oh!" I pound my fist, thinking of the Smiths being in there. I am so glad Dad is a genius.

"And two…" He sucks in a deep breath. "The helicopters are coming to run the mustangs out of the park!"

Sadie cries out, "But they'll starve!"

Her face goes white, and I can't bear the thought of the consequences either.

"Umm…" Ethan swallows hard, fighting with

the words. "We...we could feed them with the... you know."

Sadie gasps, "I thought you would never give it up!"

He shrugs. "Well, it's the difference between life and death for 243 incredible wild creatures, and it's only the difference between filthy rich and average for me."

Sadie leaps for him, nearly squeezing the life out of him with her hug. Then she turns to me, "Isaiah?"

"Oh," I wave one hand. "I'd never forgive myself if we didn't!"

She screams, and we run for Mom and Dad standing near the door.

"We overheard," Mom says. Tears shimmer in her eyes. "I am so proud of all of you. It's a yes from me!"

We turn to Dad. "You know, I can't remember having more fun than I did while hunting that treasure in...well, maybe ever. And, you know, these memories and all this time with you, that's treasure enough for me."

The roar of the helicopters grows, and soon the thunder of hooves rattles in my chest. The first horse appears, and I recognize the red-and-white stallion leaping a ditch and trying to cut to the left! One of the helicopters dodges to force him straight again. The herd moves like a river over the far side of the valley. I look over at Sadie, but she's paler than ever.

"What's wrong?" I ask, as one tear slips down her cheek as she searches the herd.

"There she is! It's Firefly!" Once again, the beautiful paint mare is very last, her tail streaming behind her at half-length, still black from the flames. I turn to Sadie. "You're not…"

She clenches her jaw, trembling. Then she spins for Ember's stall. I chase after her, my hand stops hers on the stall latch. "Sadie! Are you sure you want to do this?"

Sadie looks at me, blinking back tears. "Keeping him is the best thing for *me*. Letting him go is the best thing for *him*. He's wild at heart. He always will be. He needs Firefly!" She slams open the latch, and the sound makes me flinch.

Can she handle letting him go? Her quick movements scare Ember, and he gallops in a tight circle around the stall. All the milk he had been fed had done him good; he's full of energy and life again. Sadie dashes tears from her eyes. "See? We've gotten him strong enough to…" She chokes back a sob. "To set him free!"

She gently quiets the foal, hugging his neck one last time. "*I love you, forever and always.* Follow me, Ember!" I throw open the stall door and with a trembling hand pull out my knife with the other.

Sadie holds out one hand as if she's letting a bird perch there. When she steps from the stall, Ember sticks close to her, following her hand. As he passes me, I snatch his tail and cut off a few of the long strands. Down the long aisle, Sadie starts to run, with Ember keeping pace.

"Watch out!" I shout to my family, standing in the doorway. They leap out of the way as Sadie and Ember pass through the door at full speed.

"Sadie!" Mom cries.

But Sadie doesn't stop. She and Ember run toward the herd, far distant now.

I bite my lip. *Will they make it before the herd is long gone?*

I shout, rushing after her. Sadie seems to gain wings as they fly over the valley. Ember's tail is straight out as he gallops after her. They don't slow with the creek, leaping over it together. The image is forever seared in my mind. But Firefly is so far ahead, and the helicopters are so loud between us. Desperate, I run behind them. *How can we possibly make Firefly stop?*

If only Ember would whinny! My lungs are burning from running, and I'm falling behind Sadie's intense pace; but I force a strangled sound from my mouth. Ember's ears flick back, giving me hope.

My second whinny is still pitiful, but louder, and

probably sounds nothing like a horse. But then the most wonderful sound rips through the air!

Ember's voice is shrill as he whinnies long and loud. Far ahead, Firefly turns her head as she slows down! *She heard him!* Once more I make the awful imitation of Ember's voice, and he whinnies again, still running alongside Sadie.

Firefly skids to a halt, her ears pricking and lungs heaving. She opens her mouth, nostrils flaring as she neighs for her baby. Ember's head lifts higher still as he calls back to her. Firefly's hooves throw up clods of dirt as she bravely dodges the helicopters swooping low to force her forward.

Ember calls again, and Firefly's eyes roll white in fear as a helicopter's prop wash blows her mane wildly about her head.

"Stop!" I shout uselessly at the pilot. But a mother's heart beats strongly in the painted mustang, and she leaps straight toward the helicopter.

The pilot turns aside as Firefly gallops like the wind back down the valley, calling even louder for Ember. He's caught sight of her now! He is flying swiftly like an arrow straight toward Firefly!

He passes Sadie easily as he races for his mother. Sadie crumples into the grass, and I force myself to race to her. I slide on my knees behind her, grabbing her once again in my arms. She's sobbing hard. Tears stream down my face as we watch the horses meet. They circle each other, and Ember's mouth is open as Firefly nuzzles his neck. Sadie reaches out for him, and all I can do is hold her.

The chopper has circled around and swoops lower, driving Firefly and Ember toward the herd. Together, they run into the wilderness, their home.

-32-

"Well, it's time to leave Yosemite," Dad says. "Let's pack up."

With my shoulders slumped, I step into the canvas tent alone. With my hands on my hips, I scan the small space that feels so much like home. Leaving is always the hardest part of visiting a national park. I do a double-take when I see something shining at the foot of the bed.

"What's that?" I whisper. Moving closer, I recognize Uncle Elliot's compass now spread open, revealing all of its intricate faces.

"Where did you come from?" We hadn't seen Uncle Elliot again, though we hoped to see him soon. A public announcement will be made about the treasure and its funding of the mustangs.

I see a handwritten note on the bed.

Rawlings family,

I couldn't have pictured a better ending to my treasure hunt than my own family finding it. Your plans for its use say a lot about you all. You'll be hearing from me again.

Uncle Elliot

P.S. Isaiah, the old compass is yours. Guard it well; it's more valuable than you think.

My family walks in; and after they read the note, I pull Sadie aside. "I've got something for you."

I hold out the lock of Ember's tail. She gasps, holding it against her heart, "Oh, Isaiah!" She doesn't say anything else, but those two words are thanks enough.

"You did the right thing. Your choice was the hardest thing, but you did it," I say softly.

She bites her lip. "I'm glad he's home with his momma, and I'm so glad I got to meet him."

"And I've got no taffy left for the plane ride home! I might just starve to death on the way," Ethan complains.

Sadie rolls her eyes. "You'll be just fine."

"Ethan?" I ask. "I just have one question. Why didn't you warn us that Mr. Smith was coming?"

He draws his lips to one side, thinking hard. "Oh-uh…well about that…" He clears his throat. "You see, I was really hungry up there in that tree, and I happened to have two pieces of taffy in my pocket. And…well…I put them both in my mouth at once, and they glued it shut so I couldn't whoo…"

I smack my forehead, remembering the soft sound Dad and I had heard and imagining him desperately trying to whoo.

Mom is rummaging around in her bags. "Greg, where's my bacon box?"

Dad, Ethan, and I look at each other sharply. "Well, there's a long story behind that…"